I0611676

Kaine's Reparation

Shattered Empire, Volume 3

D.M. Pruden

Published by D.M. Pruden, 2020.

Free ebook offer

FREE EBOOK OFFER!

As a way of saying thank you for purchasing this novel, I want to offer you a free ebook.

To claim your free story please join my reader list by going to **https://www.prudenauthor.com/Kaine1-free-offer**

Unwelcome Visitor

HAYDEN KAINE HIT THE auxiliary thruster and was sucked into his chair hard enough to rattle his teeth. His shuttle's frame vibrated under the stress of struggling to escape the planet's gravity well.

He had a good lead on his pursuers, but they made up for it now. He couldn't make himself believe the acceleration of their ships. Human physiology shouldn't be able to withstand the kinds of G-forces they pulled. He realized they were being piloted by AIs, which would make his escape more difficult. Tau Ceti, like most of the systems he visited, had achieved some impressive technological advances.

A plasma burst bloomed metres from his port side. They did not miss. They were forcing him in a direction to capture him.

Like a defiant child, Hayden pushed his acceleration to the upper limit of his endurance and veered to the left. Once he escaped the atmosphere, the advantage should become his.

His drop ship was not designed for evasive combat moves. The modifications after the last few close encounters were welcome, but they were proving insufficient for the hostility he now encountered.

Another blast shook his small craft. That one had hit his armoured hull. They were no longer interested in capturing him.

A quick perusal of his readouts told him the enhanced armour held up to whatever they were throwing at him, but Hayden was pretty sure they hadn't yet pulled out their big guns.

As the air thinned in his upward climb, his pursuers dropped back, having reached the limits of their ability to follow him. The familiar tug of gravity lessened, and he heaved a sigh of relief. After adjusting his course heading to take him to his rendezvous, he glanced at the object responsible for all the drama. It was only as big as his palm, and those who dispatched the interceptors had no clue what it was, or that it even existed.

1

As far as they knew, he was a raider caught trespassing in their salvage yard. Stealing junk from decommissioned ships wasn't an offence worthy of the fuss they were putting up, but as Hayden had learned, isolation made people more covetous of any old technology. There was no way to replace anything, so old parts were particularly valuable. Most of the worlds he had visited guarded everything jealously, and few took kindly to strangers poking about.

It had taken months to confirm their target was located here and weeks longer to figure out the ship they sought was mothballed and scheduled to be cut up for parts. He was fortunate they hadn't begun the task, which allowed him to board and locate the innocuous component.

As soon as he got back to *Scimitar* and handed his contraband over to the engineers, his role in the scavenger hunt would be completed. Others could do their part and maybe—just maybe—humanity would have a chance.

An alarm sounded, and Hayden's sensor panel lit up with a proximity warning. Four patrol ships had broken orbit and were on fast approach.

Whatever he stole was not something they were willing to let go of easily. It was a lot of overkill to apprehend a single scavenger kicking around a junkyard for spare parts.

Every planetary system they had visited over the past six months had a different way of coping with the collapse of the interstellar jump gate, but one thing was common among them: they were all xenophobic in the extreme.

The once united Confederation of almost a thousand suns was fragmented, and formerly connected worlds were now isolated. Forced to rely on their own resources, it seemed a human tendency to protect whatever remained, even if it was useless.

With even the closest occupied systems years apart at light speed, humanity had been plunged into a dark age. Hayden feared what the long-term outcome would be if the situation persisted much longer.

His speakers crackled with demands for him to stand down and prepare to be boarded. He was in no mood to comply. Plotting an evasive course, he broke orbit and rocketed away from the planet.

The four pursuing ships were now joined by two more, and they were closing on him.

A red light bloomed on his console, informing him his engine was overheating. The suborbital fighters had done more damage to his ship than he'd realized.

Entering his command override, he closed the alarm down and pushed his thrust to the maximum while he still could.

Even with his intervention, the AI system would shut everything down when it reached critical temperature. There was nothing he could do to prevent that. He would be at the mercy of those who chased him. Based on their unfriendly reaction to him, he doubted they would give much credence to his reasons for violating their airspace.

Another alarm flashed, and a klaxon boomed. The ships had fired a missile. Hayden had only a few seconds to brace for impact, and he prayed his ship's hull held.

His ship shook. His engine output sputtered as it was shut down.

Now, with only inertia to carry him, he was minutes away from interception.

He mentally kicked himself. He was given the opportunity to install weapons in addition to the defensive armour. He declined because if he thought he could survive a firefight, he might be tempted to take unnecessary risks. He didn't want to hurt anyone.

Now, such naive sentiment was going to get him captured or killed when they learned his identity.

An hour from his rendezvous at full burn, there was little chance of him escaping. Activating his comms, he issued a mayday.

Pavlovich would be pissed. This was supposed to be a stealth operation. The last thing anyone wanted was to attract attention. Now, if this mission had any hope of success, he was going to need some assistance.

After a long interval with no response, Hayden repeated his distress signal.

Still no reply.

His pulse racing, he expanded his broadcast to the other channels. He didn't really care at this point if his pursuers heard him call for help.

Silence was his only reward.

The ships would be on him in a few minutes.

He tried to reactivate his engines, but the failsafes prevented him from doing so.

The speaker crackled to life, and for a moment, his heart raced in anticipation of hearing Pavlovich's gruff admonition. Instead, an unknown voice ordered him to prepare to be boarded.

Now it came down to likelihoods.

When they arrived, they would search the ship and find the pilfered component. Once it garnered the attention of the authorities, it would become impossible to retrieve. It was an outcome he could not allow.

Without the object, humanity was defenceless against a threat it couldn't imagine.

A cynical laugh escaped Hayden. There was a good chance that even with the component and what it would lead them to, humanity was doomed. He and the others had been chasing this ghost for months and were no closer to learning what the cynosure was. During that time, they had convinced themselves it was the last great hope.

Nobody really knew how it might help. So desperate was the situation, they were grasping at myths and legends.

All he understood was the Malliac horde would eventually arrive. When that happened, no one stood a chance.

He unbuckled and retrieved his prize. Pushing off from his chair, he floated to the storage locker.

Rummaging through it, he carelessly tossed items aside to drift about.

His desperation grew as his search failed to turn up the item he knew had to be there. If he got through this, he promised himself he would adhere to Cora's demands he keep things better organized.

Finding what he sought, he checked to assure himself it was charged. After setting its delay timer, he duct-taped it to the contraband component then launched himself across the cabin to the galley, even as the insistent voice over the speaker demanded his reply.

With a manic chuckle, he forced his package into the waste disposal chute. Before he closed it, he jammed other random objects in until it was filled. He had no idea if his plan would work, but the time for brainstorming was over. He heard trucking thrusters being clamped to his hull and knew his time was almost up.

Forcing himself to be patient, he waited for the right moment. His hand tightened on his handhold as he anticipated what would come next.

When the attached rockets fired to bring his ship to heel, his body was jerked forward. Only his grip on the handle prevented him from being dashed against a wall.

He pulled himself back and hit the ejection release. They'd interpret the cloud of debris escaping as damaged parts shaken loose by the braking manoeuvre.

Hayden pushed himself toward the storage locker and removed a pressure suit in case they decided not to use the docking hatch.

As he activated the HUD, a proximity alert came up. Another, much larger ship approached at high speed.

He hurried to the pilot seat and strapped himself in. A quick review of the sensors showed his captors breaking off and fleeing.

A loud voice boomed in his ear. "Your new playmates didn't stick around, Kaine. Was it something you said?"

Pavlovich had arrived in *Scimitar*, and he didn't sound pleased.

Is This Worth It?

THE PRESSURIZATION cycle of *Scimitar's* hangar had barely completed when the hatch opened, and Hayden descended the ladder. He removed his helmet and threw it across the deck.

A tall, bearded, middle-aged man entered, accompanied by a slightly built woman, many years his junior.

"What the hell, Kaine? Take it easy on the equipment."

"You certainly took your time, Pavlovich."

"What happened?" asked Stella.

"The same bloody thing that happens in every system we visit. I got shot at."

Throwing his gloves down, he stormed to the rear of his shuttle to examine it for damage.

Pavlovich joined him in the inspection. "It looks like the ship stood up to it for the most part. Still, it took more of a beating than I would have expected. What did they hit you with?"

Hayden turned on the captain. "How should I know? I didn't stick around to see what tech innovations they came up with over the last ten years."

"Why are you so angry? The armour held up."

"That is why I'm upset. If they had done more damage, I'd at least believe they had a chance against the Malliac when they arrive."

"Maybe they have something bigger. From where I watched, it looked like they were shooting to capture, not kill you."

"Oh, you saw all that, did you? Why didn't you answer my hails?"

"The FTL glitches are ongoing. We were forced to do a system-wide reboot to fix things."

"When I was in the middle of that mess?"

"It couldn't be avoided. It had to be fixed in order to come help you."

"This ship is a piece of shit," Hayden muttered.

Stella slipped an arm around his waist. "Don't let Cora hear you say that."

He sighed and embraced her. "I didn't mean it. I'm just frustrated."

"You hid it well," said the older man. "Did you at least recover the component?"

He scowled. "I'm fine, by the way."

"Yes, I know. Stella kept an eye on you the whole time. You didn't answer my question."

"Yes, Pavlovich, I found the bloody thing."

"So where is it?"

He pointed at the hangar door.

The captain stared at him, perplexed, before realization contorted his face with anger.

"Out there? Why would you do that?"

"Relax." Hayden enjoyed his moment. "I attached a delayed homing beacon to it so you can find it."

"How long a delay?"

"It should turn on in about forty minutes."

"Bloody hell," growled Pavlovich as he stormed away.

Smirking, Hayden watched him depart. "I'm not an empath like you, but I think he's upset."

Stella shook her head. "That was mean."

"He had it coming. Did you really watch me the entire time?" He pulled her close.

"You know I did, but you're deflecting. What's bothering you? You've been agitated since you departed for the mission."

He released her and went to pick up his helmet. "At first I was worried about what I would find. Every planet we visited on this snipe hunt turned out the same: civilization devolved into anarchy. Everyone is fighting for control of local resources, oblivious to the approaching threat."

"We couldn't send a warning out to every system."

"That may be true for some of the outer systems. But we sent messengers to three of the last eight we've visited. People seem more concerned with who is going to be king of the hill instead of who is coming to tear it all down. The situation is like that sinking ship analogy...what was the expression you used?"

"Rearranging the deck chairs. Hayden, what do you expect? When these worlds were cut off from the Confederation, they lost all support. Any military assets stuck in the system were all they were going to get."

"Assuming they weren't squandered in civil wars, like we've seen elsewhere."

"But there was innovation as well. We encountered new technologies. Perhaps it is like Pavlovich suggested; they possess weapons we didn't see."

"I hope so, because unless this thing we're chasing is what he believes it to be, humanity doesn't stand a chance."

· · · ·

An hour later, Hayden removed the object from its case and turned it in his hand. It looked both alien and familiar.

Stella watched him intently. "What do we even know about this? Who built it and for what purpose?"

"I told you before; nobody knows. Originally, the people who began to assemble the device this belongs to thought it would point to a portal to another dimension," said Pavlovich. "I'm not so sure. All we really understand is that it is part of a machine described by the alien civilization your father discovered."

"You think it's Glenatat technology? Is this device related to the wormhole that took us to their world?"

"It might be," said the captain.

A woman's voice came over the speaker. "A linguistic comparison suggests otherwise."

Hayden turned reflexively toward the glowing white sphere embedded in the table. It pulsed with energy as the voice spoke. "Care to elaborate, Cora?"

"I ran a comparative analysis on all the archaeological records uncovered on colonized worlds over the last one hundred and eighty years. While there is similarity between them, they can confidently be separated into three distinct language groups. The culture describing the machine this component fits is not Glenatat."

If anyone would understand their technology, it was Cora. It had saved her, allowed her mind to be transferred from her dying body, and melded it with an alien artificial intelligence. As she spoke, Hayden was disturbed that she sounded less like her old self every day. It was as if she lost touch with her humanity as time passed.

"So, if it isn't Glenatat, then which culture gave us the design?" asked Stella.

"Xeno-taxonomy is not why we're here," said Pavlovich. "All that matters is the records allowed the device to be assembled over the past seventy years. Once it is completed with this part, it will open the cynosure. That is what we seek."

"You think it is a portal?" said Hayden. "How does that help against the Malliac? When I signed up for this, you said it would give humanity access to a way to defeat them. That suggested you knew about a weapon."

"I implied. Look, those who've been chasing this thing for generations understood it pointed to a technology far more advanced than anything we can achieve in a millennium. The assholes who collected it were interested in one petty thing: taking over the Confederacy."

"But you have a bigger vision?" said Stella.

"*We* have one—all of us together. We have seen things nobody else can appreciate and taken on the Malliac—"

"And got the snot kicked out of us." Cora sounded like her old self.

"True, but we were one ship outfitted with advanced alien technology. Since our benefactors decided to go into hiding, our only other hope to save the world is to repeat the whole miracle."

"You think the cynosure will lead us to the aliens behind it so we can persuade them to help when the Glenatat were reluctant to?"

Pavlovich shrugged. "If there is a better idea, Kaine, I'm all for it."

The room fell silent. Hayden rubbed his temples to relieve his growing headache. "This always was a long shot. In fact, as we sit here debating, it sounds improbable we will find anything of use, and humanity will fall to the Malliac regardless."

"Are you saying we should give up?" said Stella.

He turned to her, and a slight smile curled up the sides of his mouth. "You once asked me if I believed in fate, do you remember?"

She nodded. "You said you didn't."

"If you consider everything that led us here...maybe we *are* fated to save humanity. I think, since we are this deep in, we must finish what we began. I can't see any other chance, and time is running out."

"That may already be the case," said Cora. "Sensors detect a vessel entering this system at ninety percent of light speed."

Pavlovich rose from his chair. "Who is it?"

"Unclear at this distance, but there are tell-tale dark energy signatures."

• • • •

Hayden reached the bridge and accessed the science station. The captain entered right behind and sat in his command chair. He hit the comm switch. "Sound battle alert. Cora, is the FTL up?"

"Yes, Cap'n, all systems are at your disposal."

"Helm, point us at that object and jump us to a position five light-minutes in front of it. Be ready to fire up the sub-light engines the moment we materialize. We need to intercept that ship."

He turned to his Gunnery Officer. "Bring the weapons online and target the vessel as soon as we arrive."

Not waiting for a response, he gave the order to activate the faster-than-light engine.

"Hang on to your stomachs, people. Here we go."

The air around Hayden crackled with static discharge. His skin crawled and vision blurred as the whine of the FTL drive filled his ears.

A blast of colour and a momentary sense of weightlessness ended with a scorching pain behind his eyeballs.

His stomach heaved, and he was grateful he'd not eaten as he heard someone else retch.

"God, I hate that," said Pavlovich. "Look alive people, you can clean up your puke later. Find the ship and bring us to an intercept course, maximum acceleration."

The crew responded like a well-tuned musical instrument, everyone attending their assigned duty despite their physical reaction to the experience. Every person reacted in a different manner, with some being more affected than others. It was nothing he could ever become used to, so Hayden kept his meals small when he knew a jump was imminent.

Within a few seconds, he was recovered and inspecting the sensor readout.

"We are receiving a stronger signal. I can identify dark matter phase distortions covering seventy percent of the vessel's hull."

"Cora, can you confirm Kaine's readings?"

"Aye, Cap'n, the XO is correct as usual."

Hayden suppressed a smile. "Its configuration is a UEF courier drone, Captain."

"Is there anything else out there?"

"No, sir."

"Assessment, Mister Kaine?"

"That much dark energy damage can only come from a Malliac weapon."

"So, wherever it came from is likely overrun. Shit!"

"We knew it would happen eventually."

Pavlovich scowled at him then turned his attention to the helmsman. "Match our speed and heading with it. I want to capture it and hand it over to Cora's engineers go over with magnifying glasses."

Kaine addressed the navigation officer. "Project its point of origin and tell us what system it came from."

Pavlovich nodded his approval and sat back in his chair, grim-faced.

Hayden knew they shared an understanding. Time was up, and the Malliac were on the doorstep.

"FIFTEEN HOURS HAVE passed. Give us the lowdown on the drone, Cora."

Pavlovich looked like he hadn't slept, and Hayden was still recovering from the effects of the FTL jump.

"Aye, Cap'n, though getting anything was a royal pain."

"Skip the whining and get to it," the captain snapped.

Shocked, Hayden turned to him but held his tongue when he saw the black mood on Pavlovich's face.

The conference room fell silent. After a significant pause, Cora resumed her report in a clipped tone. "Sixty-two percent of the vehicle had no molecular integrity due to dark energy weapon damage."

"Where did it originate, Kaine?"

"We traced it back to Epsilon Eridani."

"E-Eri is a little less than six light years from this one." The frown deepened on the captain's brow. "That means this courier drone was launched almost seven years ago. Cora, can we confirm it was attacked by the Malliac?"

"Is there anyone else besides us and them who use this kind of weapon, Cap'n?"

"That system is a bloody long way from Mu Arae; around fifty-five light years, if memory recalls."

"Yes, but the attack at Mu happened fifty years ago," said Hayden. "We've always suspected the ones we met there were stragglers." He scowled as the significance of the information sank in. "This suggests they are more widespread than we assumed."

"I can't remember how far E-Eri is from the Sol system."

"Ten and a half light years, Cap'n. That means they could be at Earth by now."

"Assuming they made a bee-line for it. I don't think it likely. Why would they pick that star for their next feeding? The Terran system may not be in imminent danger."

"Only if we assume an intentional linear advance. The timing of these attacks implies the Malliac are spread out like a cloud. I think the XO is right."

"What are we going to do?" Hayden said.

"You're assuming there is anything we *can* do."

"That's a dark thought, Cora."

Pavlovich sneered. "She's been a bit testy lately, Kaine."

"Thanks for pointing that out, *Captain*." Cora's tone softened. "I'm sorry. I don't know why I said those things."

Hayden tried to defuse the tension between them. "We're all under stress, so let's not dwell on it."

"Agreed, Kaine. What are our options?"

"Well, this suddenly makes our mission to locate the cynosure all the more imperative."

"If we aren't too late. There is no guarantee it doesn't point to anything more useful than an alien recipe book. We must consider Earth may have fallen."

"We have to do something!"

"We are," growled Pavlovich. "Cora, run a probability simulation based on our current data. I want something more than worry and conjecture to guide our next decision."

"I'm already setting it up, but there are really big error bars on the results."

"It can't be helped. In the meantime, instruct your engineers to tear the courier drone apart. See if you can recover the documents and messages it carried. That may give us a clue or two."

"I'm all over it, Cap'n."

Hayden was glad to hear Cora sounding more like her old self.

"If you don't mind, I want to discuss a private issue with the XO."

"No problem. I'll alert you when I find something. Ta-ta."

Pavlovich waited for several seconds, as if he was making sure she was gone.

"What's going on, Captain?"

"How do you feel, Kaine?"

"Sir?"

"Right now, how do you physically feel?"

"Like shit, to be honest. Headache, tired, irritable..."

"Me too. How was Stella this morning? Why didn't she join us?"

"She didn't feel too well, either. I chalked it up to the crew's emotions affecting her empathically, but now I'm not sure. Cora seemed a bit off, too..."

"Yeah, almost the entire crew acts like they spent the night partying at the Academy."

"A virus?"

"One that affects her? I don't think so, Kaine."

Pavlovich drummed his fingers on the table as he pondered the situation. "She started acting...different a few weeks ago."

"I didn't notice."

"Yeah, well, I have served with her longer than you. Trust me when I tell you she's been getting testier. It is at its worst after we make a jump."

"You suspect the FTL drive is the cause?"

Pavlovich nodded. "It's doing something to us too, though this is the worst I've felt. Surely you noticed we've been mopping up the bridge a lot more lately after we use it."

"I thought it was just my imagination."

"Well, I wish you had said something...we all should have. Anyway, the reason we were late pulling your ass out of the fire is because I made Cora run a full diagnostic on the drive."

"Did she find anything?"

"Nada, everything is in tip-top working order."

"I'll instruct the medical synths to examine the crew."

"Ensure Stella is involved. Her empathic abilities can offer some insight."

Pavlovich rose and left without another word, leaving Hayden to ponder the situation.

Until now, his first encounter with the Malliac ten years before at Mu Arae was a bad memory.

Both Sol and E-Eri were more than fifty light years from that system, in different directions. Relegated to sub-light speeds, the aliens should not have been a threat in this part of the galaxy for another few years. Until a few moments ago, there seemed to be ample time available to develop a defence against them.

Everyone he knew outside of *Scimitar*'s crew lived on Earth. He always took for granted he would return to them. Now, the prospect anyone he ever loved might be dead or on the run in deep space terrified him.

Without the jump network, there was no way to announce a system had fallen under attack except by courier drone. If the Malliac were advancing like a cloud of locusts for the past decade, consuming every Confederation world they encountered, how many countless billions were dead? The magnitude of the number was beyond his ability to comprehend.

"WOULD YOU PLEASE HAND me that regulator?"

Hayden passed the device to the android and watched it work with the dexterity of a surgeon.

The engineering avatar was the most lifelike synth he had ever seen. He could almost fool himself into believing he was working with the old Cora.

"Why are you looking at me like that?"

He didn't realize he was staring.

"There's a little something on your cheek," he lied as he leaned forward with a cloth.

"Oh, thanks. The dermal sensors aren't optimized anywhere other than the hands. Did you get it off?"

Hayden smiled. "You look beautiful."

"Still trying to see if I can blush, Lieutenant?"

"Are you finished?" He pointed to the FTL drive.

She turned back to her work. "Almost, but nothing is out of order with it. It does what the physics says it is supposed to. I can't find any reason here for what's happening to everyone."

"Well, it was worth a shot." He rose to his feet. "If it had been something we could adjust, that would be the easy fix."

She shook her head in an exact imitation of how Cora used to. "No, we are experiencing something at the quantum level the human body does not respond well to. I'll keep digging into the theory behind this technology."

"If something is affecting our physiology, it still wouldn't explain why you're displaying the same symptoms."

"It probably is related to how I was melded to Alcon. Even with almost a decade of pondering it, I still don't appreciate how he managed it."

He recalled how close she and the Glenatat AI were.

She smiled. "At least I can't puke."

They both laughed, but it died down quickly.

"Hayden, if the initial biomedical analysis bears out, we may not be able to use the FTL much longer."

He shook his head. "We can't leap to conclusions. We need to confirm there is damage happening."

"If you spent much time working with the transdimensional physics like me, the danger would be obvious to you. When we jump, we tune and split the quantum state of every atom in the ship. The entanglement—"

"I'll never understand the intricacies as well as you, Cora. If you think there is a problem, I believe you."

She smiled. "Sorry. What I mean to say is that if my theory is correct, with every hop we accumulate errors at the subatomic scale. Eventually, it will mess everything up at a level we can see."

"Like our physical and emotional state."

"Yes. Even the Glenatat bio-wafers comprising my hardware are affected."

"Didn't they mothball the technology?"

"Yes, we uncovered it in the AI records when *Scimitar* was trapped on the other side of...well, we don't know where we were. It was the first method they employed for interstellar travel. It is easy, now, to see why they abandoned it."

"How many jumps before any damage is permanent?"

"We can't say that hasn't already happened."

"You're suggesting we shouldn't use the drive again?"

She hesitated. "Given the circumstances, we should think twice before we do."

Hayden shook his head and leaned against the bulkhead. "All this time I believed we had a technology that would save the empire. I thought if we could give humanity a tool to reconnect civilization and replace the destroyed light gate..."

He fell silent, unable to finish.

Cora's hand rested on his shoulder. He looked up to see eyes almost like he remembered, but not quite human.

"I realize you had hoped this technology would redeem you from your guilt. Destroying the network was the only choice, Hayden. If those Malliac had accessed it, they could have struck any system in the empire without warning. Even a fraction of their number would have been more than humanity could have fought off. There is a fighting chance now because of you."

"I thought I accepted that. But every system we visited revealed the same thing: civil war, anarchy, chaos. Losing our connection across the stars only forced us to revert to our baser nature. Maybe humanity's time is over, and, like other dominant species, we must face our own extinction. Perhaps the Malliac are to us as the asteroid was to the dinosaurs."

"Are you suggesting we give up hope? That doesn't sound like you, Hayden."

He looked up at her and shrugged. "This morning when I got out of bed, we still had a viable plan to go to Earth, find the cynosure, and discover a way to stop them, but now..."

"That goal remains. The only thing different is an appreciation of how little time there is to achieve it."

"And the price we may all pay."

"There is a cost to doing nothing out of fear for what the FTL will do to us. The Malliac will eventually arrive here, too, and *Scimitar* cannot stand up to the full strength of their horde."

"I suppose you're right, Cora. I just..."

"Hold on!" She looked blankly into space as if hearing something Hayden could not.

"Our sensors just detected a number of ships approaching from the same vector as the drone."

The emergency klaxon sounded. Pavlovich's voice boomed throughout the ship. "Battle stations. All hands report ready status. Lieutenant Kaine to the bridge."

It had begun.

First Blood

BREATHLESS, HAYDEN burst through the hatchway. The bridge was buzzing with focused activity. Without a pause, he hurried to his station.

"There are four dark matter hull signatures entering the system," Pavlovich said. "They are following the drone we intercepted."

Hayden activated the sensor log and scrutinized the data. "The ships are all small vessels, about what we would classify as scouts."

"Maybe they were weren't trying to catch it," said the captain.

"You think they followed to see what occupied system it would lead to?"

That idea disturbed Hayden. It suggested the Malliac did not randomly choose the star systems they ravaged.

"Those were my thoughts, too." Pavlovich lifted his chin. "Cora, did you make any progress determining how they communicate?"

Her disembodied voice came over the speaker. "Sorry, Cap'n, but that nut can't be cracked with what we know."

Hayden approached the command chair. "Since they do not possess faster-than-light capability, we should assume their communication ability is also relegated to relativistic physics."

"If that is the case, they are on their own, with no backup."

"We probably should destroy them before they send back any information about this system."

A grin grew beneath Pavlovich's scraggly beard. "Itching for a fight, Kaine?"

He smiled. "It's been a while, sir. I feel like kicking some Malliac ass."

"Plot an intercept course to those ships. Gunnery Officer, warm up the rail gun and bring the dark energy cannon online."

"All subluminal engines at your disposal, Cap'n," said Cora over the speaker.

"Punch it," ordered Pavlovich.

The deck jumped beneath Hayden's feet as the gravity plating struggled to adjust to the ship's acceleration. Though the bridge temperature was cool, a bead of perspiration dripped down his cheek.

"Time to intercept is two minutes, Captain," announced the helmsman.

The hatchway opened, and Stella entered. She was pale and appeared to be in discomfort.

"Good morning, Miss Gabriel, I'm so very glad you could join us."

"Shut up, Pavlovich."

He grunted and turned to watch the image on the forward holographic viewer.

Hayden regarded her with concern. She and the captain did not get along well at the best of times, but she never was openly disrespectful. Pavlovich knew damned well how sensitive Stella was to the presence of the Malliac. Maybe his own discomfort amplified his insensitive behaviour. Whatever it was, the tension between them was unusually high.

Hayden returned his attention to the sensor readout. "The four ships broke formation. They are spreading out."

"Obviously they surmised we're not in a welcoming committee. Maintain target locks on each ship. Kaine, show me some tactical options."

Hayden directed the computer simulation outputs to the holo-projector. "Our choices are limited at this distance, but there is another problem." He pointed at the long-range field.

"What the hell is that?"

"The ships that chased me out of orbit."

"You mean to tell me the silly bastards followed us after we pulled your ass out of the fire? What did you say to piss them off, Kaine?"

Ignoring the jibe, he indicated detailed vector projections. Pavlovich studied the image and nodded as the situation became clear to him.

"The Malliac changed their course to intercept those ships," said Hayden.

"What is their crew complement?"

"They are modified corvette patrol vessels, so about thirty each."

"A hundred and twenty lives. Shit, shit, shit! They just made everything worse. Helm, time to weapons range?"

"Twenty-three seconds, sir."

"Adjust our heading to take us through the middle of those Malliac ships. Gunner, the moment they are in range, open up on the closest one with a rail gun volley. As we pass by, hit them with the cannon at twenty percent."

"That will extend the recharge time," said Hayden.

"I don't intend to stick around and trade punches with these bastards. If they are only scout ships, maybe we can finish one off quickly and the others might reconsider and retreat."

The deck plating rumbled as the first rail gun projectile was launched. Hayden's eyes were glued to the viewer in anticipation. Suddenly, the lead Malliac craft belched a fiery cloud of debris and veered off course. Seconds later, the lighting dimmed as the dark energy cannon drew power and fired on the damaged vessel.

The space surrounding it rippled with a discharge wave as the ship was twisted apart. A brilliant flash erupted, and it was gone.

Before anyone could register a reaction, the remaining three vessels scorched past *Scimitar* and were gone.

Hayden returned to the sensor readout. "They did not change course. They ignored us and are still heading toward the other ships."

"How long until they reach them?"

"They will arrive in one hour and sixteen minutes if they maintain near light speed."

"Well, shit. Cora, bring the FTL engine online."

"Cap'n, is that wise?"

"We're not leaving them at the mercy of those bastards. We need to destroy every one of them before they can return to the horde and report what they saw."

He ordered the helmsman to plot new coordinates in front of the Malliac then hit the switch to make a ship-wide address. "All hands prepare for emergency FTL transit. Everyone, grab a bucket and hang on."

Hayden looked at Stella, who had somehow managed to grow paler at the announcement.

When all stations reported ready, Pavlovich gave the command to jump.

Hayden's vision tunnelled as needles of pain stabbed at the backs of his eyes. He squeezed them shut and waited for the disorientation to end. When the wave stopped, his stomach heaved, and he turned his head to avoid vomiting on his panel. All about him he heard the splattering of sick hitting the deck, fighting to keep from heaving again from the stench. The captain was bent forward in his chair, wiping his mouth.

He mumbled, "I didn't enjoy breakfast so much the second time." Then, as if nothing had just happened, Pavlovich sat up and began to bark orders at his recovering bridge crew. "We'll try the same thing as before, so look alive."

Interposed between the oblivious human ships and the aliens, *Scimitar* accelerated toward the approaching Malliac.

The ship was rocked by enemy fire. Not strapped in, Hayden was knocked to the floor to land in a puddle of his own puke. Retching, he wiped the offending matter from his shoulder.

"Put your harness on, Kaine, and pull your shit together. Tell me what's going on."

As he buckled in, he wondered why Cora did not call out the situation report.

He read the summary aloud. "Minimal damage to forward rail gun port number one. It is still operational."

"Is that all they have?" Pavlovich wore a delighted smile. "Send those bastards our reply."

The lead Malliac ship exploded, and its companions returned fire on *Scimitar*.

The harness dug into Hayden's shoulders as they were buffeted about by the assault.

Seconds later, the alien ships shot by and continued toward the approaching human vessels.

"Cora, what is our status?" called Pavlovich.

There was an uncomfortable pause before she responded. "I... uh, give me a sec, Cap'n..."

Frowning with concern for her, Hayden read from his display panel. "Stress damage to forward dorsal hull. Minor buckling of armour near engine number three, but the substructure is unaffected. Rail gun number one is offline."

"We're lucky these assholes didn't send the 'A' team."

"Good thing we reinforced the plating over key areas." Cora sounded more like herself. "I'm still worried about—"

"If it isn't mission critical, it can wait. Let's rack 'em up and do this again."

A crewman groaned but stopped after the captain scowled in his direction.

"Cap'n, I'm concerned about the wisdom of doing this."

"Duly noted, Engineer. Prepare the drive for another jump. Helmsman, you know the plan."

"Ready for your command, sir."

"Everybody hang on to your cookies." Pavlovich nodded to the helm officer, and *Scimitar* jumped.

. . . .

Startled, Hayden's eyes suddenly shot open. He had no recollection of the FTL hop happening, but a quick glance at the recovering people around him told him it must have taken place. Everyone was disoriented. Stella was collapsed on her couch, eyes closed and possibly unconscious. Before he could release his harness and go check on her, Pavlovich spoke. His voice was weaker than normal and hesitant.

"Status review; all stations report in."

As the crew groggily tried to comply, Hayden pulled himself together and checked his panel readouts.

"Sir, if this chronometer is correct, we've all been unconscious for over a minute."

"What? How could that...? Never mind—where are the Malliac?"

"They are still on the same approach vector. Time to weapons range, two minutes, thirty-four seconds."

"Holy hell! Helm, get us moving, Gunnery Officer, prepare for another salvo."

Seeing the helmsman's condition, Hayden unbuckled and rushed to him. After inputting the commands over the still disoriented man's shoulder, he turned to Pavlovich's empty command chair. A movement in the corner of his eye drew his attention to the gunnery officer's alcove, where the captain now sat.

He shouted, "Be prepared to respond to what they do. There isn't much time."

Hayden nodded and directed the helmsman to move to another seat. A wave of dizziness washed over him, and he shook his head to clear it. His eyes focused on the tactical display as the realization struck him this might be their last chance.

"Is full power available, Cora?"

"She's occupied, Kaine."

"Captain, I have an idea. Prep the aft rail gun."

"What are you thinking?"

"No time to explain. Just be ready to go with it."

"Aye-aye...*Captain*."

Hayden hit the ship-wide address switch. "All hands: prepare for emergency acceleration."

He fired the manoeuvring thrusters and rotated the ship while pushing all four engines well past the red line to maximum output. The force sucked him back into his chair while *Scimitar* threatened to shake herself apart. The gravity plating could not keep up, and the field collapsed, sending loose objects hurtling to the back of the bridge. Hayden hoped everyone had heeded his warning and strapped in.

He called over the building whine of the straining engines, "They should be coming up fast."

"Yeah, I'm ready," replied Pavlovich.

There was no usual rumbling of the deck plating as the aft rail gun fired. Hayden transferred the sensor readout to the helm station. The lead Malliac ship veered off course, plasma spouting from its engine section. The lighting dimmed as power was drawn for the dark energy weapon. A moment later, the damaged vessel vanished, engulfed in a distortion field.

The remaining vessels opened fire. *Scimitar* shook and several panels overloaded.

"They've disabled our rail guns," said Hayden. "They're coming around for another pass. Man, I can't believe the G's they're pulling."

"What is our status?" said Pavlovich.

"Engine number four is compromised, and I need to shut it down."

"Not yet!" shouted Pavlovich. "I just need a few more seconds to recharge the cannon."

Hayden ground his teeth as time seemed to slow.

Scimitar lurched, and his panel lit up. "Engine four is down; two is failing..."

Pavlovich's response was to fire the weapon. The lights went out and stayed off. The space around the final Malliac exploded in a brilliant flare of rippling light.

Once he had assured himself it was gone, Hayden shut down all engines but one and began to slowly decelerate the ship.

A large hand pressed down on his shoulder, and he looked up to see a relieved Pavlovich, smiling at him.

"Excellent work, my boy."

He collapsed in his command chair and hit a comm switch.

"Cora? Are you there, girl? Talk to me."

Silence.

"Cora!"

Time is Up

KAINE STOOD BESIDE Stella's bed in a medical recovery suite.

"Hayden, I'm fine."

"Bullshit, you were the only person to lose consciousness. I want you checked out."

"The medi-synths ran every known test on me." She sat up and placed a comforting hand on his arm. "There is nothing wrong."

"Nothing they can determine." He fell silent.

"I'm sure she'll be okay."

Pavlovich approached the chair. "Who will be okay?"

"How is Cora?" asked Hayden.

The captain looked from one of them to the other, concern etched on his face. "She's recovering. There are no more Malliac signatures in the area and your pursuers lost track of us when we jumped. It will take them some time to find us. Cora's taking some alone time in her VR and assures me she is fine."

"But you don't buy it," said Stella.

"Do you? We were hit hard, and nobody is acting like themselves. Cora's personality changed the most. She's never retreated into herself like this."

Hayden turned to Stella. "Can you sense what is going on with her?"

She shook her head. "Everyone's emotions flooded me like a tsunami, and I'm still hypersensitive. The doctors gave me a mild sedative, but it dulls my empathic ability. I can't distinguish individuals. Cora was hard for me to read before this happened."

"I should go visit her," said Hayden.

"In her VR world?" said Stella. "She's been after you for months to do that, but do you think now is the appropriate time?"

"Feeling a little jealous?" Pavlovich was smirking.

She glared at him. "Shouldn't you be somewhere else?"

Hayden frowned at them. "If I were incapacitated, I would want a visitor."

The captain shrugged. "Then, by all means, if your woman okays it, I'm sure Cora won't object."

Stella exploded at him. "Must you be such a misogynist?"

He gave another shrug. "A weakness of mine; I see a button and I push it."

"Well, if you don't want me to clock you, leave me alone."

Pavlovich lifted his hands in mock surrender. "Okay, I get it. I'm sorry. Though, in my defence, all of us are acting out of character."

"You've always been an ass."

He raised his eyebrows and turned to Hayden. "And on that note, I suddenly recall a need to check in on Engineering. Your little trick stressed the engines, and I want to make sure Cora's boys and girls know what they're doing. We are going to be relying on them more in the future."

Hayden frowned. "Why would we do that?"

"I was going to wait until Stella recovered before I call a staff meeting..."

"I'm fine, let's discuss it now."

He nodded to the medical synth. "Please give us some privacy?"

The android acknowledged and left the suite.

Pavlovich paused to gather his thoughts. "I reviewed the data the engineers pulled from the drone. Things are bad."

"What did you learn?" asked Hayden.

"The Malliac are deeper into Confederation space than we feared. Two years before E-Eri was attacked, they began to receive courier reports from a dozen neighbouring systems. All of them reported being invaded by an unknown, overwhelming force. In no case did additional reports follow."

"Holy shit."

"With the new information, our computer model paints a pretty grim picture. Seventy percent of confederacy worlds have or will soon fall to the Malliac. This system is within weeks of invasion. The main force isn't far behind the scouts we toasted."

"Any news about Earth?"

Pavlovich shook his head. "The simulation gives a ninety-two per-cent probability it hasn't fallen yet, but things don't look good. The best scenario predicts they won't reach Sol for another two years."

"And the worst case?"

"The most likely timing has them arriving there in eight months."

Stella said, "You didn't answer the question. What is the worst-case projection?"

Pavlovich's shoulders slumped. "Sixty days."

Silence fell as they digested the information.

"We have a critical decision to make," said Hayden.

Stella stared at Pavlovich. "You don't want to go to Earth. You are thinking about running. Even without my ability, I can sense that in you."

Hayden turned to the captain. "Is this true?"

"It is one option I am considering, yes."

"How could you do that?"

"It is my job to ensure the survival of my crew."

"What about your duty to the UEF?"

Pavlovich snorted. "There is no more United Earth Federation, Kaine. Every system is isolated. Those we've visited are in anarchy or fighting civil wars. Only thirty percent of the empire remains, and the number shrinks by the day. We have to weigh the gain against the risks."

"I can't believe what I'm hearing. We possess everything we need to find the cynosure and—"

"—and what? All we know is it is somewhere in the Sol system. If we all live through the jump there and avoid being shot at, we still have to locate the damned thing. That job alone could take years."

"So you just want to turn your back on everything and head for the hills? Where do you propose we run?"

"People have been known to survive a Malliac incursion." Pavlovich directed his attention to Stella. "We have our own early warning system. She and her father hid from them for years at Mu Arae."

"That is an existence I never want to face again."

"But it can be done. The way I figure it, our odds of survival are better if we find an asteroid to park behind here than jumping into the fire by going to Earth."

"If your hide is what you're worried about saving, you can always find a rock to cower behind there," said Hayden.

"Assuming we don't die when we use the FTL to transit there."

"What are you talking about?"

"I dug through Cora's research," said Pavlovich. "I don't pretend to understand what half of it means, but the little I do frightens the shit out of me. The Glenatat drive is tearing us apart with each jump, creating irreversible havoc to every molecule of *Scimitar* and us. We didn't detect anything because things tend to swing back toward normal as time passes between hops, but not completely. The effects are cumulative. Our last succession of jumps cascaded them from one hop to the next, damage accumulating on damaged atoms with every leap. If we had made another one..."

"Why is it affecting Cora so much more?" asked Stella.

"That one is a mystery, even to her. Maybe the components housing her consciousness are more sensitive. My point in all of this is even if we survive another jump, I'm not sure she can. And without her, we can't run the ship."

Despite his words, Pavlovich could not conceal that his concern was not with the ship's functioning. He had a soft spot for her. The two of them shared an almost familial bond, like the one between father and daughter. Stella told him she noticed it long before.

She spoke softly. "What are her feelings about it?"

"I… I didn't discuss it with her. She's not in the best frame of mind to make that kind of decision."

"Why are you speaking for her?"

Pavlovich's face reddened. He struggled for the words. "I almost lost her once."

Stella's hand rested on his shoulder. "Yegor, you can't decide for her, as much as you want to."

"I just…I can't bring myself to ask her. I'm afraid she'll choose to put herself at risk."

"Do you want me to ask her?"

"I'll do it," said Hayden, "because, if we are going to abandon Earth and what remains of the Confederacy, I want to hear her decision with my own ears. That way I will be sure it is what she chooses." His eyes locked on to Pavlovich's.

"Fair enough," said the captain. "Just promise me you won't attempt to influence her."

"I would never do that."

"You may believe that now, Kaine, but your family is back on Earth. That's more than most of the rest of us can claim. If she tells you she doesn't want to do it, are you prepared to accept that? You won't want to persuade her to change her mind?"

He noticed them studying him for the truth of his response.

"I give you my word."

Pavlovich extended his hand. "Then I'm satisfied for you to be the one to speak with her."

Hayden accepted the captain's hand.

He hoped if it came down to choosing between keeping his promise and letting everyone he knew face certain death, he could make the right choice. Stella did not look happy.

Strange Reality

"THIS FEELS WEIRD."

The sun visor on Hayden's modified helmet was lowered, and he couldn't see a thing. "You're sure this works?"

"Don't be such a big baby, Hayden." Cora's voice came through the helmet's speaker. "The captain uses it all the time."

"Pavlovich visited your VR?"

"Why do you find it so hard to believe?"

"I don't know. He just doesn't strike me as the 'come-over-for-a-coffee' type."

Cora's melodious laugh filled his ears. "There's no coffee involved, but I take your point. There is a lot more to him than he presents."

"I'm beginning to see. What now?"

"Now, you sit back and try to relax."

"Nothing good happens when you're told that. Remember your last visit to a dentist?"

"Don't be silly. This doesn't hurt...much." She giggled.

Smiling at the return of her sense of humour, he leaned back into the chair and released his death grip on its arms. He didn't realize how nervous he was. "Now what?"

He suddenly had the sensation the floor beneath him had vanished, and he floated in black, empty space. The cool air blowing across his face smelled faintly of lavender, Cora's favourite scent.

"Cora, what's happening?"

"Relax, you're in."

"Why is everything black?"

"Give it a moment. I'm easing you in one sense at a time, so you aren't overwhelmed. Ready for some colours?"

He smiled. "Sure."

An explosion of every colour imaginable surrounded him. He squeezed his eyelids shut, but it had no effect.

"Try to relax, Hayden. I'm adjusting the optical nerve stimulation to match your brain pattern."

"My God, that was bright. Is Pavlovich blind or something?"

"Everyone is different. How are things now?"

The smart-ass reply vanished from the tip of his tongue as his vision came into focus. What he saw overwhelmed him.

The riot of random colours had resolved into an idyllic pastoral setting. He was in the middle of an endless field of young wheat. The green, supple shoots waved in unison with the soft breeze caressing his face. The fresh scent of ozone after a thunderstorm filled him with childhood memories of vacations with his father he forgot ever happened. Dark storm clouds retreated over the horizon, unveiling a brilliant evening sunset.

"Cora, this is beautiful. What is this place?"

"Proxima Centauri b, where I grew up."

Hayden continued to drink in the vista. "It reminds me of one of my grandfather's homes on Earth I used to visit as a boy. Where are you?"

"Turn around."

He turned to see a young, slightly built woman. Cora's face was as he recalled from a decade ago, softer and more expressive than her impressive android body. Her long blonde hair was done in a braid, which cascaded over her shoulder. Instead of the coveralls he associated with her, she wore a long, pale blue diaphanous gown.

"Wow, you dressed up for me," he said.

A panicked thought came to him, and he checked his own garb to discover a freshly pressed standard duty uniform.

She giggled. "Relax, silly. Of course you're wearing clothes. What must you think of me?"

"I would blush if I could."

"You can. You're in control of your avatar's response in here."

"This is a new look for you...I'm—"

"Surprised? There is a lot you don't know about me, Hayden."

"I'm beginning to realize. I'm sorry I misjudged you."

"Oh, don't be ridiculous. Everyone shows one face to the world and keeps another secret."

"Then I am honoured you are sharing this part of yourself with me."

She smiled and turned to a knoll a short distance away. "Shall we go for a walk?"

He joined her, and they strolled through the swaying young wheat shoots. As they walked, he continued to glance at her.

"You imagined you'd find me as a scruffy, blubbering lunatic in a padded cell, didn't you?"

Taken aback, he stammered, "No, nothing like that. I was unsure what to expect."

"But you are concerned about my mental health. Cap'n Pavlovich is."

"We all are, but you appear fine to me."

They stopped at the top of the hill overlooking a verdant valley. A small settlement was at the bend in the river below, and he guessed it was her childhood home.

"Retreating to here helps me heal, but I still feel unsettled outside of this."

He was at a loss for words, so he remained quiet and took in the scenery.

"I know why you're here, Hayden."

"Cora, I'm sorry my visit isn't under other circumstances."

She returned a wan smile. "May I be completely honest with you?"

"Of course."

"I'm afraid of what will happen to me if we make another FTL jump. When I leave this place and return to *Scimitar*, she seems different to me. It's like I can't gain a stable footing on a rocky cliff path, and with one wrong step, I will plunge into an abyss. It is almost as if the world I occupy is torn apart a little more with each transit."

"How long ago did this start?"

"I noticed changes, cracks, after the very first jump."

"Why didn't you say something?"

"They healed, or at least at first they seemed to. By the time I realized the damage was permanent, we had a mission to accomplish. I thought I could compensate and fix things. I can't."

She looked at him, her sky-blue eyes sad. Hayden was shocked to feel tears running down his cheek. He wiped them away and coughed to conceal the act.

"I saw the projections. If something isn't done, the Malliac will overrun and destroy what remains of humanity. The cynosure is our only chance, it's just...I'm really scared, Hayden."

He took her hand in his. It was surprisingly cold.

He understood why she retreated to this world. If he had the opportunity, he would do the same. Her fear was understandable, and he identified with it. He didn't know if his emotions were influenced or created by the VR, but he was confident the Cora he knew would not stoop to that.

When he thought about it, what he experienced here was familiar. He pushed it to the back of his consciousness in the real world. Here, he had no inhibitions and was free to explore his true emotions. He thought it had the potential to become addictive.

"I should share something with you I'm ashamed of. I promised Pavlovich I would not attempt to influence you, but I came here open to doing so anyway. But I just can't ask you to sacrifice yourself, Cora. You've given far too much already. We will find another way."

She smiled. "Reverse psychology, Lieutenant?"

He held up his hands in protest. "No, I mean it. I repent of that intention. Perhaps humanity's time in the sunshine is over. Maybe we need to accept that and live out the rest of our lives with those we love."

She squeezed his hand. "I now should be honest with you. Before you arrived, I decided I want to help. We should make the FTL jump to Earth."

"But it could kill you, or—"

"Or worse? I considered that. In fact, I calculated five hundred and seventy-one possible outcomes and their respective probabilities. I still want to do this."

"Why?"

"Are you a religious person, Hayden?"

"Not really. I believe in a higher power, in whatever form it may take, and I hope there is something after this life, but my family never attached much value to formal religion."

"Well, mine did. I was raised as an old-time Roman Catholic, complete with the guilt..." She pointed at the settlement in the valley. "Right down there. When my little brother died, I lost the faith and left home to join the UEF. My parents were very disappointed."

A tear ran down her cheek as she looked up to the emerging stars peeking out of the darkening sky. "Proxima Centauri fell to the Malliac. It was in the reports the drones carried to E-Eri."

"Cora, I'm so sorry."

"This place is all that remains of my home, my family, and the only other home I ever knew aside from *Scimitar*."

She lowered her chin and faced him. "I don't want that to happen anywhere else. I don't want you, or Pavlovich, or anyone to have nothing left but memories and an empty feeling there was nothing you could do to help save them. I won't be responsible for that."

"Cora, you should consider..."

She held up a hand to stop him. "Please don't patronize me. I know what I am choosing and the reason why. It comes back to how I was raised down in that village, and something I learned when I was a little girl. It always stuck with me, and I never believed it to be true until now."

"What is it?"

"A line from the Bible: 'There is no greater love than to give one's life for another.' I don't remember the exact quote, because memorizing scripture isn't a Catholic thing." A shy smile spread across her face.

"Cora, I don't know what to say."

"Don't say anything. If I can't spend my life for a chance to save the lives of the people of Earth and the other systems not yet invaded, what is my purpose?"

"WHAT THE HELL DID YOU say to her, Kaine?"

He and Pavlovich were on their way to the conference room.

"Believe it or not, I tried to dissuade her."

"When Cora contacted me, she said there was a solution. What did she tell you about it?"

"Nothing," said Hayden as they entered the meeting room. "This is all news to me."

Stella was already at the table, in quiet conversation with Cora's android. He was taken aback at first sight of it. Despite its sophisticated design, her machine body now appeared more artificial to him since he encountered her in VR.

Pavlovich took his seat. "I'm glad to see you up and about, Cora."

The android's facsimile of a smile only made Hayden's uneasiness greater.

"What's wrong?" whispered Stella as he sat next to her.

His gaze lingered on Cora as she conversed with the captain. "Nothing important. I'll tell you later."

"Okay, Engineer," said the captain, "tell us why we are here."

"Well, I assume the XO already told you of my decision. I want to make the jump to Earth, but there are a few technical issues we need to address."

"Like finding a way to keep you from dying."

"Since my meeting with Lieutenant Kaine, I reviewed the Glenatat archives housed in Alcon's original AI matrix."

"That is where you discovered the plans for the FTL drive?" said Hayden.

"Yes. Before the machine merged with Cora, it decrypted its database. It contains millions of records that are of limited use to us because we can't translate them. We should have kept your father with us, Stella."

"I doubt that would have helped, Cap'n. Most of the information is in an ancient dialect predating the ruins Doctor Gabriel studied on Mu Arae."

"What did you discover in your search?" asked Hayden. "Something helpful, I hope."

"I came across some documents explaining why the Glenatat abandoned this tech."

"I'm guessing it was because it was killing them," said Pavlovich.

"That is the executive summary, but the details I could translate are more revealing. What is happening to us is related to the inability of the engine to exploit quantum entanglement while transferring through dimensional—"

"Whoa, girl," the captain raised his hands. "Nobody here possesses a PhD in transdimensional whatnot. Dumb it down for us, please."

"Sorry, sir. Copy errors happen at the subatomic level when we transit with the FTL drive. Of course, they accumulate, and because the hardware housing my consciousness is less complex than biological material, I am affected more."

"How does any of this solve how to keep you alive if we make another jump?" asked Stella.

"Well, it doesn't, but I came up with an idea that could work. If we construct a new matrix for me out of raw materials, I can transfer over to it. That should protect me for a few jumps until we come up with a permanent solution."

"Sounds reasonable. However, I sense a 'but' coming," said the captain.

Cora laughed. "You know me too well, Cap'n. Yes, there is a problem. One critical component needed is constructed of dark matter, which we don't have."

Stella's forehead creased. "I don't understand why you are laughing. That is a pretty insurmountable barrier."

"Actually, it isn't," said Hayden. "We can recover some from the wreckage of those Malliac ships."

"Didn't our weapon destroy most of it?" asked Pavlovich.

"We don't need much, Cap'n, only a couple of milligrams. There will be enough trace amounts from what's left out there."

"We can't so easily build everyone else a new body," said the captain. "What about our damaged cells?"

"And *Scimitar*," added Hayden.

"The damage to the ship is easier to address. My techs run metallurgical analysis of *Scimitar*'s structural integrity after every jump. I project she can survive up to five more transits before the hull, and any non-Glenatat instruments become compromised."

"What about the armour?" asked Pavlovich.

"Its degradation is less predictable. I wouldn't count on it surviving beyond two more jumps."

"That will be a challenge when we encounter the Malliac."

"Can anything be done about what is happening to us?" asked Hayden.

"I conferred with the medical synths who are examining the crew. Organic matter seems to behave elastically and repairs itself to a degree, but there is still a cumulative change."

"How can that be?" said Stella. "An atom is still an atom. Why would organics be more resilient?"

"They shouldn't be," said Cora, "but the evidence still suggests it is so. There is a lot I can't fathom about the physics. The math to understand the Glenatat research isn't invented."

"The question is," said Pavlovich, "if we can build you a new matrix, and *Scimitar* won't fall apart, will the rest of us survive an FTL jump to Earth? That is kind of critical."

"I can answer once data is gathered from the medical samples. I should have a better idea in about three days."

"Let's proceed as if your analysis will tell us good news. Mister Kaine, order a course plotted to the closest Malliac wrecks. We'll begin work on your new home right away, Cora."

Bad News

WHEN THE CAPTAIN'S call came, Hayden and Cora were in the middle of the delicate process to extract and stabilize dark matter from the debris of the Malliac ship. Though she assured him she had everything in hand, he was reluctant to leave. He wanted to do more than be a concerned friend. Volunteering to be her assistant in the complex procedure of rebuilding her Glenatat AI matrix was the best way he could think of to show his support.

The truth was, they both knew he was out of his depth, and she was too polite to tell him to go do something else. When the captain requested his attendance at an urgent meeting, it saved both the embarrassment of her sending him away to get him out of her hair.

The door to Pavlovich's cabin opened, and Hayden was surprised by Stella's presence. She perched on the edge of the bunk while he leaned against the desk. Hayden's arrival had interrupted what appeared to be a deep conversation.

"What's going on?"

"Come in, Kaine. There are some things I want to discuss."

Pavlovich invited him to sit next to Stella. She was pensive and avoided eye contact with him as he joined her on the cot.

He towered over them, stroking his beard as he assessed them both. Hayden felt like he did as a boy when called to his father's study.

"Is something wrong?"

In answer, the captain scowled and grabbed a pad. He perused it for a few seconds before handing it over.

Stella didn't appear to be interested, as if she was familiar with its contents.

Hayden scrolled through the document. "This is the summary of the medical tests."

"You don't need to pore over the data, just skip to the conclusion."

He skimmed, then went back and carefully reread the information a second time.

"It says we all experienced chromosomal damage."

"That is what we all share. Beyond that, everyone is affected in a different way. In some, like yourself, if you read further, the impacts are minor and can be corrected. In others, things are more dire."

Hayden poured over the litany of woes. As Pavlovich had indicated, some of the crew only suffered from changes easily treated, even aboard ship. Some of them, however...

"Cancer? How is that possible? Nobody's contracted that for at least a century."

"Well, it has appeared in ten percent of us, including me."

"The condition is treatable, right?"

Pavlovich shrugged. "I'm told the tumour in my brain is only half the size of the one on my liver. It is such an exotic disease that I need to seek help at a specialized research clinic. I heard there is a good one on Earth."

"Did you receive a prognosis?"

"Yeah, I'm going to die, but not necessarily from the nasty thing in my body. The Malliac may finish the job before the cancer can."

"That is terrible news."

Hayden looked to Stella, who continued to stare at the floor. Seeming to sense him watching, she looked up at him. "I'm the same as you; no significant damage."

"Then what's wrong?"

She looked to Pavlovich, an eyebrow lifted.

"Don't look at me. I don't even understand why you told me before him."

"What is he talking about, Stella?"

She sighed. "I was pregnant, Hayden."

He blinked, confused.

"Was?"

"I lost it after the last jump."

"I... I'm so sorry..."

"It was for the best. There were deformities...the child couldn't have survived."

He put his arm around her shoulder. She shrugged it off and stood. "Can we please get to the purpose of this meeting?"

Hayden frowned but decided to hold his tongue.

Pavlovich said, "Stella recommends after everyone receives their report, a vote be held."

"Some of us can clearly survive at least one more jump," she said. "Some, however, suffer from more dire conditions. Another could exacerbate things, or even kill them."

"Before you ask, Kaine, I agree with her."

The ship was already on a skeleton crew. Even if Cora's plan for her new matrix worked, *Scimitar* wouldn't be able to function in a conflict with the Malliac if they lost many more.

He was at a loss for words.

"Don't get your knickers in a knot, son. I'm going to Earth to see this thing through, and I'm confident most of our crew will make a similar decision."

"How about you, Stella?"

"I'm not sure." She turned to Pavlovich. "Please excuse me."

Without awaiting a response, she left.

"Give her some time, Hayden. She needs to deal with her own stuff before she is in any condition to handle everyone else's reaction to their reports. It will be overwhelming for a bit."

"I'm sorry, I didn't think. How are you doing?"

"I'm dealing with it, but it isn't the most important issue to address. How are Cora's modifications coming along?"

"What? Oh...everything is proceeding as planned. She should return with the material in another hour. After, it will take two days to complete the construction and test its operation."

"There isn't a lot of time. I want you to put your diplomatic training to work. Contact the planetary government in this system and warn them of what is to come. Share everything with them, including sensor logs of what happened here."

"Without our sensors, they can't even see the Malliac. They won't believe much of it. Certainly not enough to prepare a mass evacuation plan."

"We can't hold everyone's hand. Tell them everything, and after, it is up to them. Since the jump gate collapse, they might be prepared to accept what you tell them."

Hayden was at the door when Pavlovich said, "I asked her to come see me."

"Sir?"

"I read the medical report, and I asked Stella to come see me. I... had to share my shit with someone. That was when she told me about the loss of your child."

"She didn't tell me she was pregnant."

"I'm sorry you had to find out like this, son. I wish I could give you some time together to deal with this, but..."

"We will do what is necessary," said Hayden, and he departed.

He stopped ten paces down the corridor. He knew he should feel some sense of loss, but he couldn't drum up any emotion except annoyance. Why had Stella not shared news of her pregnancy, and why had she confided in Pavlovich, not him? And he couldn't understand why she shut him out a few minutes before. Did she somehow blame him?

His selfish concern embarrassed him.

Had she sensed his feelings before he even realized them for himself? If she had, and now faulted him for those emotions, it would be unfair.

He shook his head. He was being ridiculous.

She wasn't like that. On the contrary, she tended toward compassion and forgiveness far faster than he.

No, it was something else. He needed to find her to hash it out, but she made it clear she was in no mood to be around him now.

Scowling at his helplessness, he stormed down the corridor toward the bridge.

Perhaps the locals would be easier to communicate with.

"I CAN'T BELIEVE IT!"

Hayden hurled his headset down, eliciting attention from everyone on the bridge.

"Is there a problem, Mister Kaine?"

Embarrassed by his outburst, he walked to the captain's chair to speak with him.

"It is the locals. It took me the better part of two days to find someone who will even talk to me, and..."

"Do they think you are pranking them?"

"Yes, even though I used your priority communications ID, damn it!"

Pavlovich suppressed a chuckle.

"You find this amusing?"

"I'm sorry, it isn't funny, but it was entirely predictable. When you think about it, these people spent the last decade hammering out a local functioning government. For a long-absent representative of the UEF military to arrive on their doorstep with dire tidings probably ruffled some feathers. How much were you able to tell them about the situation?"

"I didn't get far."

"Because you're trying to talk to the wrong people. You think by reaching out to the local king of the hill, you are taking the shortest route to lighting a fire under their butts. That approach worked in your diplomacy classes at the academy, but it doesn't amount to much out here in the real world. Trust me, I know how most of these assholes think."

"So, what do you suggest?"

Pavlovich lifted his chin. "Cora, where are those local ships on their way to greet us before the Malliac happened along?"

"They turned around after they lost us on their sensors when we made our first jump. They are about forty light minutes away, heading back to the inner system."

He turned back to Hayden. "That is who you should be talking to."

He shook his head. "It makes no sense. None of those captains is in a position to prompt an evacuation alert."

"You need to think like a ship's commander on patrol duty. A bogey you were chasing suddenly vanished from your sensor lock. It was no malfunction or a ghost signal, because you also picked up a transponder signature. Now, aside from the mystery of how a ship like ours showed up in the system, you are faced with the brain twister of where the hell it went, and we didn't just disappear from one set of sensors, but from those of two other ships. They would have swept the area and found no debris, so what do you suppose their next action would be?"

"Report the incident to someone higher up the ladder." Hayden began to understand the captain's reasoning.

"Right, so now the entire local command structure is scratching their heads wondering what it all means. If, like most of the other systems we've visited, tensions are high between them and their nearest neighbours..."

"They might be worried about an invasion from them! They are already primed to listen to our story."

Pavlovich touched the tip of his own nose. "Bingo! Give the man a prize."

"I'll send them a UEF coded info burst. If I throw in our sensor logs of the battle and other background information—"

"Whether they believe you or not, their attention will be yours. Problem solved."

Hayden frowned, feeling foolish. "You could have said something earlier."

"Sorry, I had other things on my mind."

"Speaking of which..." He raised his eyebrows in silent question.

Pavlovich looked about the bridge, then rose from his chair.

After transferring command to the helmsman, he indicated Hayden should follow him. The two men walked out the hatchway and down the corridor in silence until they arrived at the conference room.

"Cora, what is the state of your modifications?"

The translucent sphere in the centre of the table pulsed as she replied. "Everything is tested and looks as good as it will ever be."

"When do you want to do the transfer?"

"If you don't mind, Cap'n, I'll wait until after the vote."

Pavlovich frowned. "Really?"

"Yes, sir. I thought it might help those sitting on the fence to hear me cast my support to go along."

A smile spread across the captain's lips. "Thank you, Cora. May Kaine and I please speak now?"

"You bet."

He leaned against the table's edge and crossed his arms over his chest. "I appreciate your discretion back on the bridge. To answer one of your questions, I'm dealing with my issue. The medical-synth supplied me with some drugs he assured me will slow down the growth of the tumours."

"A lot of people are struggling. At least five approached me to ask for advice on how they should vote this afternoon."

"What did you tell them?"

"The same thing you said when you made the announcement. I told them to decide what they can live with, and nobody will think ill of them if they choose to leave the ship."

Pavlovich nodded, seeming distracted. "What about Stella? What will she do?"

He shook his head. "We haven't spoken. I can't find the right moment. She's been working overtime counselling crew members. We have not seen each other for more than a few minutes, and when we do, she's exhausted."

"Sounds like you are both avoiding the issue."

"Probably."

"In all honesty, Kaine, without her ability to take on the Malliac I don't like our chances. I would feel a whole lot better if she was as determined as you and me to see this through." Pavlovich raised his hands. "I'm sorry, it isn't right to put a guilt trip on you. We all must accept her decision and make the best of things if she decides to remain behind."

Hayden scowled, clenching his jaw tighter.

The captain studied him. "Am I wrong to believe you will see this through? If she votes to stay, are you planning to join her?"

"What the hell am I supposed to say, Pavlovich? We were going to have a child I knew nothing about. She is grieving, and something else is occupying her thoughts. How can I compound that by abandoning her?"

Suddenly, he realized what bothered Stella, and he felt like an idiot.

"You appear to be experiencing an epiphany," said the captain.

"If you don't mind, I'll see you at the vote in two hours." He walked to the door.

"Kaine."

He turned around.

"I don't need to remind you what is at stake, do I?"

Pavlovich appeared old and worn out. His beard was greyer than Hayden recalled seeing before, and his uniform was wrinkled, like he'd slept in it. For the first time since they met, he seemed vulnerable.

"We don't know anything about the cynosure except the rumours you were told years ago. We could be making a leap that, if it doesn't kill most of us, will certainly maroon us in the Sol system until the Malliac come to finish us off. Is that the place we really want to be? Given what we've encountered on every other planet, do you think Earth will be any better? If we locate this mystical...thing and it leads us to technology that can help, I worry what is left of the UEF will be in no condition to effectively use it. This all may be a lost cause. Maybe it would be best if we picked a star as far away from here as possible and made our final leap."

"Of all people, I expected you to be the most determined to see this through."

"You mean given my upbringing and the role I was raised to fulfill? I suppose that was the case not long ago. But recent events make me question whether anything can be restored, or if it is even worthy of being saved."

"That is fatalistic crap. We've only visited a handful of systems."

"Yes, but the same thing happened in each. When the light gate collapsed, it was like the thing unifying humanity and elevating us from savagery suddenly ended."

"The situation has been difficult for everyone since the collapse, but that is only a technological hiccup. We solved the problem once, and I am confident we can do it again. With time, we will fix the FTL issues and use the technology to reunite the Confederacy."

"All we will confirm is without the dominating presence of a central government and its ability to militarily enforce its will on the colony worlds, the idea of a united civilization is a fantasy. Without a big stick held over our heads, our nature makes us little more than warring clans fighting over resources."

"What are you saying with all of this philosophical musing, Kaine? We aren't worthy of surviving? We should roll over and accept our extinction? That is what we are facing; the end of the human species."

"I'm just telling you I have doubt. Maybe this is a fool's errand, and my time could be better spent finding a quiet place to live out my life with Stella to raise children."

"What point is there to that bucolic dream? When the Malliac arrive, your family, if they survive, will be among the last humans scattered across the galaxy. Do you think you can all find each other and begin rebreeding a threatened species?"

"Everything comes to an end, Pavlovich. Everyone dies."

"I don't for a minute accept this is our time, any more than I believe the cancer in my body is a death sentence. But I am not going to argue with you. Go speak with your woman. You can both tell me your decision at the vote."

Hayden nodded and turned to the door.

Pavlovich spoke to his back. "Regardless of what you decide, Cora and I are going to at least make the attempt to save humanity because that is what we think is right."

"I would expect nothing less from either of you, Captain."

He left to find Stella.

Losses

HAYDEN PAUSED OUTSIDE the door to his quarters. He realized Stella sensed his approach when he left Pavlovich. It would be difficult for her not to; he was an emotional mess, pulled in too many directions.

That was probably the worst condition he could be in to talk to her. He had learned if he kept his feelings from getting the best of him, she was not impacted and became free to be herself. When he ran hot, however, his emotions tended to dominate their interaction, and she allowed herself to be pushed to the background, as if she feared confronting the emotional maelstrom he sometimes nurtured.

He closed his eyes and deepened his breathing to slow it and become centred.

The door opened, startling him.

Stella stood on the opposite side of the doorway, wearing a wry smile.

"You felt me coming." Hayden's face warmed.

In reply, she took his hand and led him inside.

The lights were dimmed, and strategically placed candles cast a warm glow about the room. Two glasses of wine were poured and waited for them on the table. She picked them up and handed one to him.

"What is the occasion?"

"I owe you an apology. I'm sorry I shut you out and didn't tell you about the baby."

He smiled and clinked his glass with hers. "Thank you."

He joined her, sitting on the edge of the bed, afraid of saying something stupid and breaking the mood. As if reading his thoughts, she squeezed his hand.

"Hayden, I only learned I was pregnant that morning. In all honesty, the loss of the child before I could accept the reality of its existence was overwhelming. I needed to work through my own feelings and

59

come to terms with what happened, all while the emotions of the crew demanded my attention with increasing urgency. I was afraid I wasn't strong enough to deal with your reaction, so I kept you distant and in the dark. It was selfish and wrong in so many ways."

He took her glass and put it aside with his before he embraced her. He held her tight as she buried her face in his shoulder. After a long interval, she disengaged and wiped her eyes.

"I don't want to sound like an insensitive clod," he said, "but I am still not sure how I feel about it. I'm sorry, but it doesn't seem real to me."

"I understand." She smiled.

"I'm glad for this chance to talk, though. I was worried there was a gulf growing between us and didn't know how to cross it, or if you wanted me to try. But I realized how self-centred I was. I spent all my time focused on the goal of getting home, and I assumed you were of the same mind. When you shut me out, I reevaluated my priorities and I just want to say—"

"Hayden, stop."

"Why? What's wrong?"

"I want to be many things to you; your friend, lover...guiding conscience..."

They both laughed at the truth of it.

"But I don't want to be the reason for your decision to return to Earth."

"What are you saying?"

"I want you to decide without regard to what I might choose."

"Do you want to remain here? If so, then I—"

She raised a hand. "That is what I am talking about. You are ready to go if I should elect to go with you, and you are prepared to abandon the mission if you believe I want to stay behind."

"Well, which one is it you want?"

"I'm not going to tell you."

"What the hell? Why not?"

She stood and walked to the table. "During that short time I was pregnant, I began to entertain the notion another future might exist for us. I never considered raising a family as a possibility for me, but the more I thought about it, the warmer I grew to the idea."

"Then it is settled. We will pack up the shuttle and make our way to another star system, away from the Malliac."

"No, because that is not your destiny. It never was."

"I told you once before, I don't believe in the crap about the plans my family had for me."

"But you do. I heard you discuss our plan to return to Earth, locate the cynosure, and find a way to save the remains of the empire. You may say you don't care, but that is not the truth. If you were to abandon that and flee with me, you would regret it forever. It would drive a wedge between us and ultimately destroy us."

"Then why don't you...?" Realizing what he was about to say, he clamped his mouth shut and looked away from her.

"I could decide to go with you and release you from the burden of making that choice, but there is a problem. I am not sure that is what I want. I think a part of me wants to vanish into the void, flee from people and their emotions; run far away from the bloody Malliac and the prospect they might be unstoppable. I don't want to face the possibility of ending my life watching everyone I love die horribly. I'm sorry, Hayden, but I am not the pillar of strength you think me to be. I am a coward."

Tears blurred his vision. "Please tell me what to do. What can I do to make you happy? I'll do it."

She approached him and held his hands. "I want you to make the right decision for you. I will make my own after you cast your ballot. Yes, I am being selfish, and what I say hurts you. I can feel it, and it is tearing my heart apart. But it can't be helped. You cannot be burdened by caring for me. You must be free to do what is required. The mission is that critical."

"Pavlovich will be disappointed. He was counting on your ability to fight off the Malliac."

She smiled. "I may decide to come, but as with you, it should be a decision made without emotion, and right now, we are too closely tied."

"It sounds like I'm being cut off again." He tried to smile to blunt the words for himself.

"How would you feel if I swallowed my own fears, hopes, and doubts? If I make the noble sacrifice, and you one day discover what I turned my back on, how would you react?"

He thought about it. "It would kill me. I think I understand."

She leaned over and kissed him on the cheek. "There is only an hour before the meeting. We've both got a lot to consider."

Time to Decide

THE SHIP'S MESS HALL was the only place large enough to accommodate the entire crew. The tables had been removed and the chairs were arranged in rows facing the back of the room.

Hayden was among the last to arrive. He was not surprised by how subdued everyone seemed. He fielded a dozen last-minute questions from anxious people, struggling like him to make the right choice. All he could tell them was to make a decision they could live with. None of them seemed pleased with his advice, but it was all he felt he could say.

He still struggled with his own resolve. In good conscience, he could not urge anyone to follow Pavlovich when there was a significant chance he might opt to remain behind. In his eyes it would compound his betrayal if he did that.

Avoiding eye contact, he proceeded to his expected place in the front row. The only seat remaining was next to the captain, who sat next to Stella.

She reached out and clasped his hand as he passed her. A weak smile tried to form on her face, as if to encourage him. Her eyes told him how difficult it was for her to retain her composure when her empathic sense was pummelled by all the raw emotion from the crew.

It was no wonder she was considering remaining behind. The intensity of emotional bombardment she would be forced to endure if she joined the expedition would be unrelenting. He didn't think he had what it took to deal with that, and he had no idea how she coped. The more he thought about her situation, the more he admired her strength and sympathized with her desire to be alone.

After he settled in his seat, Pavlovich acknowledged him with a brisk nod and rose to face the gathered crew.

"I'm not going into a big preamble. We're all aware of why we are here."

He paused and took several tense seconds to study the faces in the room. Hayden was the last one he considered, and as he did so, the captain's brow furrowed.

"Most of you were not with *Scimitar* when a vote like this was last taken. Ten years ago, your predecessors on this ship unanimously chose to leave the safety offered by the Glenatat. They risked themselves for the sake of the empire, and almost everyone lost their lives. But their sacrifice was not in vain. The Malliac were stopped in their tracks. We need to stop them permanently this time."

Hayden stared, shocked by Pavlovich as he spoke. If he was trying to drum up enthusiasm, he was doing a lousy job.

"Now, I can't expect the same from all of you. Many of you are civilians who joined up out of a sense of adventure or need. *Scimitar*'s old crew, those heroes, were all UEF soldiers. Every woman and man honoured the vow they took when they entered the service, paying the ultimate price by doing so. I am proud to have served with every one of them." He looked at Hayden.

"If we are to proceed to Earth, we require a minimal crew complement. That can only happen if enough of you vote to go. Some of you asked for advice and direction about what I want you to do. Obviously I want you to join the mission, but I can't direct you to do that. You must all make the choice your conscience demands of you."

Hayden snuck a peek behind him to see how the people were taking to Pavlovich's speech. Everyone was riveted. Some were visibly burdened with the weight of the decision they yet had to make. Others expressed determination in the set of their jaw, while fear was in the eyes of only a few.

"I do not want to put anyone on the spot. I would be lying if I told you I have no expectations of some of you." He glanced once again at Hayden. "But what I want is not important. Only you can decide how you wish to spend your life. There is a significant chance we will not survive the transit, let alone what is to follow. Still, I am determined to lead the way."

He pulled a ballot from his pocket. "I hereby make it known that I am electing to return to the Sol system to locate the cynosure, and, by God's grace, discover a means to prevent the Malliac from overrunning the cradle of humanity."

He went to the large cooking pot on the table behind him. Dramatically, he held his ballot over the opening for all to see and released it to fall inside.

Replacing the lid, he faced the room. "Take your time. After you cast your vote, you may leave the room to await the results elsewhere."

He swallowed, and tears glistened in his eyes. "Regardless of what happens, I am proud of this crew. It is an honour to act as your captain."

Pavlovich bowed his head and proceeded up the aisle and out of the room.

Hayden overheard Stella's whispered comment to Cora. "That was a bit heavy-handed."

As if in reply, Cora's android rose and walked to the makeshift ballot box. Without hesitation, she deposited her slip of paper. As she turned to leave, she paused and said for all to hear, "I'm with the Cap'n."

She then smiled at Stella and Hayden before walking swiftly for the door.

Seconds ticked by in silence before another man voted. He was followed by a woman, and two more people were on her heels to add to the pot.

At irregular intervals, people stood and cast their vote, until the mess hall emptied.

Hayden focused on the floor in front of him, struggling to avoid looking at Stella, whom he could see in his peripheral vision. After their emotional conversation earlier, he didn't believe he could make the choice demanded of him if he saw her face.

It crushed him to think he might be casting a ballot that would separate them. Even if he followed his heart instead of his gut and voted to stay behind, she had left room for the possibility she could still elect to go to Earth. The worst tragedy he could imagine was if he decided to stay, only to discover she had made the opposite decision.

Of course, if that happened, he had the option to amend his vote, but the damage would be done. His relationship with Pavlovich would be injured, and trust would be lost. That would be a critical weakness when they were in the flames of what was to come. The slightest hesitation to rely on each other could spell disaster for all.

He had probably already become a disappointment to his captain.

When *Scimitar*'s old crew was faced with the moment the captain referred to in his speech, Hayden was the first to leap to his feet and declare support for the mission.

Back then, he encouraged Stella to remain behind with her father, because he could not bear anything happening to her. She would hear none of it. Now, however, things were different.

For ten years they had scratched out a life together, believing all that time that *Scimitar* had been destroyed. The weaker aspects of his character were revealed, and she made the hard decision to leave him. Rightly, she had determined that only he could make the choice to live the life he was meant to. She would not permit herself to become his crutch, because if she did, he could never rise to his potential. Her love for him was strong enough to let them part. Now that they were reunited, as much as he never wanted to experience that sense of emptiness again, she was forcing him to face his fears and fulfill his purpose.

And then there was the baby.

Even as the revelation that they had conceived a child was followed by news of its loss, a spark of joy and wonderment was struck within him. It changed the way he perceived himself and opened his mind to the possibility of becoming a father and raising a family with her.

He wanted that.

But Stella was wise beyond her years. Aware of the change in his desires, he realized she was also familiar with his struggle with what she called his unfulfilled destiny. She sacrificed once before out of love. She would not hesitate now to do so again.

A hand gently touched his shoulder, rousing him from his musing.

He looked up into her eyes, realizing she'd deposited her ballot while he was lost in thought. She softly kissed the top of his head and whispered, "Do what you must."

Then she departed, leaving him the last person in the room.

The die was now cast.

As long as he continued to hesitate, like Schrödinger's cat in the box, both possibilities coexisted; he could be together with her on the ship or on some yet to find haven. Now that she had made her choice, everything had collapsed and he was faced with the naked gamble of guessing her decision.

It was impossible to get it right.

By trying to second-guess Stella to be with her, he would sacrifice too much of himself. By focusing on that dilemma, he disregarded the thing her resolve was intended to point him at.

She was right.

There was no choice to make.

As much as he wanted to fight the concept, every event in his life had brought him to this crux. His only decision was whether or not to take up the torch and do what he was meant to.

It sounded vain. But his father had believed in Hayden's destiny, as had his grandfather.

Stella did too, for some reason of her own.

He had fought against believing in it for so long that resistance had become second nature. It was an indulgence nobody could now afford.

He did not know what his role in the future would be, only that there was one for him to play.

Hayden cast his ballot.

He would go to Earth.

Going Home

HAYDEN STIFLED A YAWN. He was nearing the end of his duty shift, and Pavlovich would soon arrive to relieve him.

Everyone was forced to double up on duties following the vote. Most of the remaining crew was only getting four hours of sleep at a time.

Those who elected for the mission were a few more than the minimum required to operate *Scimitar* in a combat scenario. While relieved at that result, Pavlovich did not hide his disappointment that so many more decided to remain behind.

Hayden couldn't blame them. They were all civilians and didn't sign up for the conflict that was to come. Their adventures had been exciting, some of them had told him, but they couldn't justify the further risk the FTL drive put on their lives.

Some, like Pavlovich, had developed life-threatening health conditions and said they wanted to live out the days they had left before the Malliac eventually arrived. Others, less fatalistic, hoped to find a way out of the system and try to stay one step ahead of the invading horde.

In the end, there was no single correct decision, since every path had risks and most ended up facing the same result. These people had elected to eliminate much of the uncertainty the upcoming mission presented.

Perhaps they were the braver ones. He couldn't judge any of them. He nearly chose to be among their ranks instead of occupying the command chair, wishing for a cup of hot coffee.

As if by magic, the scent of his favourite mocha wafted up under his nose.

He started, realizing that he had emerged from that misty place between awake and asleep. Stella grinned as she presented the steaming mug to him.

"You were dozing," she said as he accepted the beverage and tried to hide his embarrassment.

"I had trouble dropping off on my sleep shift."

"You were snoring soundly when I got in."

He smiled sheepishly and took a sip. He'd considered sneaking one of Stella's mild sedatives but decided it would make him too dopey.

"If this coffee doesn't do the trick, I may need some stimms from medical."

"We're low. A lot of people are running on too little sleep."

"And it will only get worse from here on," said Pavlovich loudly as he approached them.

"We will need to take that into consideration," she said. "People will make mistakes working fatigued."

"It can't be avoided," said the captain as he shooed Hayden from the chair. "Cora will keep a wary eye on critical systems as a backup. Besides, it is only until the last group leaves the ship. After we make the jump, we'll be home and it should be easier for a bit."

"Until the Malliac come," said Hayden.

"If they aren't there already. If that is the case, well, I don't want to die in my sleep. I doubt most others will either."

"Actually, that is how I want to go."

Pavlovich narrowed his eyelids as he considered him. "Don't be a pussy, Kaine."

Hayden's retort was cut off by Stella. "You look well rested, Captain."

"I can drop off anywhere, something I learned early in my spacefaring career."

"Do you give lessons?" asked Hayden.

He regarded the cup in Kaine's hand. "Stop drinking that shit, for a start."

"I'd rather die than give up my coffee."

His mood sobered when he realized death might come sooner than any of them wanted. The three of them became quiet, as if sharing the same thought.

"What is our status, XO?"

"The drop ship is loading in the hangar. The transport will arrive for them in the next half hour."

"Oh, while I think of it, congratulations on negotiating that with the locals. It makes our job a lot easier."

"Once the area commander verified our sensor logs, it wasn't difficult to instil a sense of urgency in her. Hopefully there is time for them to organize a system-wide evacuation."

"I hope that is what they do," said Pavlovich. "If the stupid bastards decide to reenact the battle of the Alamo..." He shook his head. "Our people may wish they stayed with us."

"The matter is out of our hands," said Stella. "Maybe, if they see us leave, it will convince them to take the wiser path."

The captain grunted. "You are not taking into account the pig-headed nature of military commanders. If someone high enough in rank decides by holding off the invaders it will make them a hero, these people are screwed."

"Let's hope it doesn't come to that," she said as she turned to leave.

· · · ·

An hour later, the drop ship was finished shuttling evacuees and had returned to its berth in the hangar.

"All stations report ready for departure, Captain," said Hayden.

"Cora, how do you like your new digs?"

"You're funny, Cap'n. The FTL engine is spun up and at your command."

Besides Cora's new core matrix, every medical precaution possible had been taken to mitigate the anticipated effects of jump space on everyone else. There was still a significant chance that the transit would make things worse or even fatal. For a man facing what he did, Pavlovich looked relaxed.

Despite the glib behaviour, Hayden detected a hint of trepidation when the captain spoke to Cora. They were all concerned about what might happen once they made the jump, but Pavlovich appeared more worried about her than himself.

"Helm, I believe you know where we are going," said the captain. "Drop us near the old light gate."

"Aye, sir," said the helmsman, "the coordinates are laid in."

Pavlovich's cheeks puffed as he exhaled. He hit the button on his chair to address the crew. "My brave companions, we are about to make the most significant interstellar transit in human history. Our actions from this point on may well determine the fate of our species. Many of you are tired, but fight through the fatigue and perform your duties to the best of your ability. Humanity is counting on us. Make secure for FTL jump."

He deactivated the intercom and looked at Hayden. "A bit too heavy, perhaps?"

Hayden smiled. "It will sound good in the historical records."

Pavlovich shook his head and addressed the bridge crew. "Okay, people, keep those barf bags handy. We just cleaned this place up. Let's do this."

The familiar wave of disorientation and nausea washed over Hayden as the FTL drive was activated.

Seconds that seemed like minutes later, everything came back into focus. He regretted drinking the coffee and struggled to keep his stomach contents in place.

One or two people retched, but it seemed that most of the crew had heeded instructions to not eat anything beforehand.

He looked over to Pavlovich, who, though pale, grinned back. "I told you that shit was no good for you."

"Shut up," muttered Hayden as he resumed his station and examined the readout. "We've arrived on target near the Sol light gate. No ships are in our immediate vicinity."

"Thank goodness for small mercies," said Pavlovich. "Cora, are you still with us?" There was tension in his voice.

"Aye-aye, Cap'n. My systems appear fine, but I started a diagnostics run."

He hit the intercom button. "All stations report your status to Mister Kaine."

He paused a moment.

"It won't be long before we attract attention from Sol defence forces. As far as things go, we are supposed to be a UEF vessel with a military crew. It is time to begin acting like it again. For those of you who are civilians...keep quiet, do what you're told, and we will get through this."

Pavlovich deactivated the comm. "Cora, keep an eye on the long-range sensors. XO, what are the incoming reports looking like?"

"Most are green, but we've had one casualty, and three others are being transferred to sickbay." He was worried about Stella until her report came in from Medical.

"Cap'n, I'm registering something," said Cora. "Three ships departing Titan and heading our way."

"What is the ETA for the welcoming committee?"

"They are burning hot, so it will be soon. I estimate two hours if they ramp up to maximum."

"Any communications from them?"

"Nothing yet, sir," said the comms officer.

"Keep an ear on all available channels. They may have changed things up."

Pavlovich leaned on the arm of his command chair and stroked his beard, deep in thought. He caught Hayden's eye and motioned him to approach.

Keeping a low voice, he said, "What are your thoughts, Kaine?"

"By now, news will have arrived from some of the fallen systems. Our arrival spooked them. They will proceed with caution until they can verify our transponder code."

"Then their biggest questions will be if the light gate network is functioning, and how."

Hayden nodded. "We should still prepare for the possibility they will fire on us once they see our modified hull."

Pavlovich raised his chin to speak. "Cora, what is our defensive status?"

"I'm still running tests, but the initial results confirm our fears. Our armour integrity is degraded. We won't be able to take on any Malliac ships."

"What about nukes and rail guns?"

All eyes on the bridge turned to him.

Cora paused. "We can still withstand a direct hit, though we will rely on the inner hull to protect us from radiation. As far as rail guns, a close quarter impact in the right spot could do us in. I strongly advise we don't put ourselves in that kind of position."

"If that happens, it will be their call, not ours. Communications Officer, start sending friendly greetings with our identification tag."

He turned back to Hayden. "Are you still of the opinion that full disclosure is our best course of action, XO?"

"After we tell them everything, we can locate and activate the cynosure."

"You decided to be optimistic, eh? I want to see what happened here politically before I open the kimono."

"Our institutions are strong. What we saw in the outer systems will not happen here."

"I hope you're right, Kaine. If we have to start shooting back, we made the wrong decision to come."

Hayden tried to find a response but came up empty.

Pavlovich raised an eyebrow. "Yeah, that's what I thought. Cora, spin up the FTL drive in case everything goes sideways. Helm, plot a jump back to where we came from and be ready."

"Sir?" said Hayden.

"If we are blown out of the sky before we can even tell them about why we're here, we won't do anyone much good. If they open fire, we'll hop to safety and come up with a new plan."

"Assuming we survive the transit."

"In all honesty, if it comes down to that, everything is pretty much pooched."

Hayden straightened. "It will not come to that."

"Sir," said the communications officer, "the lead ship acknowledged and confirmed receipt of our identification tag. The captain wishes to speak with you."

"So far, so good," he said to Hayden before he addressed the bridge crew. "Okay, let's talk to them. Everyone try to remember what a UEF officer behaves like."

The holographic display at the front flickered, and the image of a woman in her mid-fifties resolved. She wore the standard UEF uniform with insignia of a fleet commander.

Hayden was relieved that things had not changed.

"Marlene Sulley, what a sight for sore eyes you are," said Pavlovich, wearing a huge grin.

The woman did not share his enthusiasm and retained a cautious expression. After a short transmission lag, her eyes widened in surprise and she responded. "Yegor? Is it really you?"

"In the flesh."

Another delay ensued. "So your transponder code is real, then? You *are* aboard *Scimitar*. How is this possible? The last I heard, you were fifty light years away at Mu Arae."

"It's a crazy story..." He glanced at Hayden, who rechecked his instrument panel and shook his head.

"How about you take your missile lock off my ship and I explain everything?"

"I really want to hear that tale, Yegor, but my orders give me no latitude. You're targeted until you surrender command to my boarding party when we arrive. That isn't going to become a problem, is it?"

"Are you serious?"

"I'm afraid so, old friend. A lot has happened."

Pavlovich forehead creased. "It seems I have no choice. We will comply."

Sulley seemed satisfied with the answer and ended the transmission.

"Deactivate all weapon systems and power down the jump drive," he ordered.

"What is the plan, Captain?" asked Hayden.

"Marlene and I go back a long way. I trust her. Her tolerance for bullshit from central command is very low; probably the reason she's not an admiral by now. But she's still in the fleet, so that is a good sign. Besides, they didn't start shooting first, so our plan is still in play."

"If you say so..."

"I do."

Pavlovich stared at him for a moment. "But just to be on the safe side, please call Stella to the bridge. I'll want her reading on Marlene when she arrives."

"Yes, sir." He wondered how much good Stella's gift would do them if this was a trap.

His instruments attracted his attention and showed him the other ships had begun their deceleration burn.

They would find out soon enough.

Defender

HAYDEN CONSIDERED THE drab walls of the sparsely furnished, windowless room he occupied and wondered how badly he was screwed.

When he and Pavlovich greeted the party that came aboard *Scimitar*, his trepidation about how the surrender of command would go didn't come close to what happened.

Instead of an officer entering to present his credentials and assume control of the ship, the airlock hatch opened to an armed squad of Imperial Marines.

Ten of them stormed through and fell upon them without uttering a word. Before he realized what was happening, his face was pushed roughly to the deck and his arms bound behind his back. Pavlovich was slapped into restraints but without being subjected to the same indignity of having his nose driven into the floor.

Hayden thought he was familiar with the captain's temper, but the vitriolic stream of curses he hurled at the squad commander was like nothing heard from the man before.

Without mention of what they were charged with, they were herded back to the docked transport. Separated to opposite ends of the craft, they had no opportunity to compare notes or discuss what had taken place.

They removed Pavlovich to the command ship and took Hayden to one of the accompanying vessels.

His every question was met with stony silence as they led him to the ship's brig and placed him in isolation. He had no idea if anyone else had been arrested, but after not very long, the engine vibrations informed him the vessel was underway.

Hours later, he was again transferred to another shuttle and taken down to a planet. In the dead of night, he was hustled into a detention facility and locked in a cell.

All of that took place two days ago.

At least that was his estimate, based on the number of food trays delivered to him since his arrival.

The only reason he knew he was on Earth was its familiar pull of gravity. The guard synths that brought his meals were programmed not to respond to his questions.

He thought the least they could do was give him a window. He hadn't laid eyes on Earth's blue skies for more than a decade, and the thought of a wall separating him from fresh unrecycled air irked him more than anything else.

A beep from the locked door roused him from his thoughts. A quick glance at his untouched breakfast told him it wasn't time for his meal tray to be removed. He rose from his bunk to greet this new visitor, hoping he might finally learn what the hell was going on.

The door opened, and an officer entered, carrying a briefcase and dressed in the uniform of the military legal office.

It took him a few heartbeats to recognize the man.

"Kyle Loram?"

His academy roommate and best friend was gobsmacked.

"My God! It really is you."

They stared at each other for several seconds before he advanced and drew Hayden into a brotherly embrace. Hugging him tightly, he said, "We thought you were dead."

Unable to find words that did not sound trite, Hayden held his tongue.

Kyle grasped him by the shoulders at arms length and studied his face. "They told me it might be you, but I didn't believe them. Where have you been?"

"It's a long story, but first, can you tell me what the hell is going on? Why was I arrested?"

Kyle looked at him as if he believed he was, if not deranged, then confused. "Hayden, you are facing a number of charges, not the least significant of which are impersonating an officer and high treason."

The words were like a splash of icy water on his face. The treason charge was anticipated. It had been the only plausible explanation for his incarceration, but...

"Impersonating an officer? Are you serious?"

Kyle pointed at the insignia on Hayden's collar. "You wear the uniform of a full lieutenant in the UEF. You were commissioned with the rank of second lieutenant—"

The expression on Kyle's face and the ridiculous nature of the charge forced an explosion of laughter from him.

"Pavlovich gave me a field promotion ten years ago. I haven't thought about it in ages."

His old roommate frowned. "*Scimitar*'s log entries can confirm that, but that doesn't detract from the seriousness of the other charges."

Hayden took a step back and gave his friend's uniform the once over. "Why are you here, Kyle?"

"I'm assigned as your lawyer."

"You? How the hell did that happen? When we were in school, all you could talk about was working your way up the ranks to a command position."

Kyle's frown deepened. "The collapse of the jump network altered all that for me. It changed a lot of things for everyone." He smiled. "I sometimes find it hard to believe I ended up in the MLO."

"Okay, I'm sorry for sounding so incredulous, but how did you come to be my legal defence? Isn't that some sort of conflict? Not that I'm complaining."

"I asked to represent you."

Hayden was confused. "You said that up until you saw me, you didn't believe I was alive. Why—?"

Kyle held up a hand to stifle questions. "There were stories circulating around the office about someone claiming to be you arriving aboard a ghost ship. I wanted to verify it for myself, so I volunteered."

Hayden rubbed his left arm. "They took enough samples from me when they locked me in here to positively identify me."

Kyle shrugged. "Records can be faked. It happens a lot. people trying to impersonate prominent citizens assumed trapped elsewhere when the network went down."

"Me? A prominent citizen?"

"With your family background, you're asking me that? C'mon."

"Well, I don't think of myself in those terms. Who the hell would want to pretend to be me, anyway?"

The colour drained from Kyle's face. "Oh, you don't know. Of course...how could you?"

"What's happened?"

"Your father...he's dead."

Hayden felt like he was sucker-punched in the gut. His legs wobbled as his friend led him to sit on the edge of the bunk.

"Dad's gone? How? When?"

Kyle hesitated, a pained expression on his face. "It was a shuttle crash four years ago."

"I can't believe it. We didn't part on the best of terms."

"Your disappearance affected him. After the gate collapsed and we learned of the messages you sent back to warn us about it, he took comfort in the belief you died defending the Confederacy. He was proud of you."

"You were in contact with him?"

Kyle nodded. "I visited him to deliver your things. We became close. He sort of...adopted me as your proxy."

Hayden forced a smile. "Thanks for being there for him."

"It was difficult for all of us. Katie took the news of your death especially hard."

"Really? I got the impression she wasn't too fond of me when I left."

Kyle frowned. "You treated her like shit. Dumping you was the smartest thing she could do, but don't for a minute believe she wished you harm."

Hayden's cheeks warmed. "I'm sorry; that was thoughtless. Ten years is a long time." He thought of Stella and what her admonition would sound like. "I moved on and didn't give much thought to how any of you might take my presumed death."

"I'm glad I was wrong about it."

"Does she know that I'm here?"

Kyle hesitated. "The situation with Katie is...complex. A great deal changed after the disaster. There was a coup. The would-be junta was led by our old nemesis from the academy, Admiral Thomas."

"Pavlovich was right, then. What do you mean by 'would-be'?"

"They couldn't consolidate their hold on key positions. A counter movement within the bureaucracy thwarted them until a group of loyalist generals was able to topple them."

"And what happened to Thomas?"

"He died in the final struggle and took a lot of good people with him."

"Wait a minute. Katie's his granddaughter. She would not have had anything to do with this."

"She's had it rough. She was eventually cleared, but she's under close surveillance because of her relationship with Thomas."

"Thank God she's okay. Where is she now?"

"Um, I think she's still working in the technical advancement division. She lacks the autonomy she once enjoyed. Still, she's managed to distinguish herself, but it took a long time before people stopped viewing her with suspicion."

"Do you think she'll see me? I owe her an apology."

Kyle shrugged. "I haven't spoken with her about you, so I can't say. But even if she wanted to, she won't be permitted to see you. Conventional thinking is that you were sent by Thomas to the Mu Arae system to destroy the network and create the opportunity for him to overthrow the government."

Hayden's mouth dropped open. "And you believe that?"

"Before you say anything else, as an officer of the court I am obliged to report anything you tell me unless—"

"What the hell?"

Kyle spoke over his protest. "Unless you assign me as your solicitor. Then everything you say will be held in the strictest confidence. Do you, Hayden Kaine, accept me as your council?"

"Of course I do."

"I need a formal—"

He scowled, impatient. "I, Hayden Kaine, do hereby request you to act as my legal representative."

"Good." He reached for his collar and depressed a small pip that Hayden didn't notice before.

"You were recording us?"

He pulled over the chair from the small desk and sat. "It was the only way they would allow me to see you. Now that we share solicitor-client privilege, you can speak freely."

"You don't believe I was Thomas's agent?"

Kyle shrugged. "You must admit, your situation looks pretty damning. You were called to his office, graduated early by him, and sent off on a mission to Mu Arae that resulted in the opportunity for his betrayal. When we received news of your intention to collapse the light gate system, it was viewed as the lynchpin in Thomas's plans."

"The Malliac were about to exploit a weakness and use our network to invade. It was the only way to stop them."

"So you claim."

"Didn't the Glenatat ships that transported our messengers tip any-one off that we *might* be telling the truth?"

"Malevolent, invisible aliens swarming systems and destroying everything in their path...given what happened here, that sounds like a pretty lame story."

"It's true, damn it! They can't be seen because they are composed of dark matter. We included all the details, including logs of our first encounters with them. Surely the messages on the courier drones from nearby systems are convincing enough?"

Kyle nodded. "And we can use all of that evidence to build our case."

Hayden stood and glared down at his former roommate. "Don't you people understand the gravity of the situation? They will swarm every planet in the Confederation. They are within weeks of arriving here. There is no time for this. Is nobody taking the threat seriously?"

Kyle gestured for him to calm down. "The first thing we need to do is have these charges dropped. After that, we will be in a better position to make your case that the aliens are a real and imminent danger."

Hayden threw up his hands and paced the room. "I don't believe what I am hearing."

"It is the best we can do at the moment, Hayden."

"How long will all of this legal bullshit take?"

"A few months. I can probably argue for your release to my custody under house arrest."

"Kyle, we don't have that kind of time. The Malliac will be here long before this goes to court."

"If they are as formidable as you suggest, why did you come back here?"

"The means to defend Earth from them is here. We came back to find it."

"What is it?"

"I...I don't know."

Kyle raised a skeptical eyebrow. "Okay, where is it kept?"

Hayden's shoulders slumped. "I don't know that either."

"None of this is helpful, unless you intend to plead insanity."

"You have to believe me. Hundreds have died to possess this device already. It is an alien technology discovered over a century ago. All but two of its components were surreptitiously brought here and reassembled. The last two pieces are on board *Scimitar*."

Kyle did not appear convinced. "Who is behind this secret project?"

Hayden hesitated. "That is problematic. It was under the direction of Admiral Thomas."

Kyle sighed. "You had better consider an insanity plea, because if any of your story is true..."

"Yeah, I'm screwed."

Long Lost Relatives

A KNOCK ON THE DOOR surprised Hayden. He was accustomed to his gaolers entering unannounced and Kyle using the buzzer.

When the knocking persisted, curiosity overcame reticence.

"Come in."

The door opened, admitting a man of about sixty years. His neatly coiffed hair was snowy white, and the well-tailored business suit on his tall frame seemed out of place in the military prison. His commanding posture gave the impression he was someone used to having his way. That would explain his ability to gain admittance to such a secure facility. Something about him seemed familiar to Hayden, but he was unsure why.

"Can I help you?" he said, rising from his bunk.

The distinguished stranger studied him for several seconds, then nodded his approval. "So you're Amelia's son."

Hayden's mother died when he was six, making him unaccustomed to people associating him with her instead of his well-connected father.

"I'm sorry, but have we met?"

A wry smile spread across his visitor's face. "No, but I've known you since you were born. I'm your mother's brother, Eli Gordon." He extended his hand.

Hesitantly, Hayden accepted the handshake while he studied his would-be uncle. He didn't attempt to mask his skepticism about the man's claim.

"I don't recall anyone ever mentioning you."

"I would be surprised if you did. Your father and I weren't on friendly terms because of my objection to his amorous interest in my little sister. After they were married, he made it clear I was not welcome in the Kaine home."

"Let's assume I believe you. Why are you here?"

Eli nodded and produced a business holo-card. "I'm with your legal team. The firm I run consults to the Military Legal Office. My genetic profile is on record with them if you wish to test my claim or my credentials."

"I just may do that," said Hayden as he pocketed the card.

He offered the man the lone chair in the cell.

"So, 'Uncle,' I'm sorry to disappoint you, but I'm already assigned a lawyer."

"And a damned fine one he is. I trained him."

Hayden frowned, confused.

"I should clarify," Eli said, "I am also a retired instructor of the academy."

"That explains your connection to the MLO."

"When your file fell into Kyle's lap, he asked me to advise him."

"Does he know we are supposedly relatives?"

Eli smiled. "We *are* related, and no. But when he confirmed you to be Amelia's boy, I could not sit on the sidelines, especially given the nature of your case."

"The fact that a long-lost relative is involved was just icing on the cake, I suppose."

Eli laughed, exposing straight, white teeth. "I'm sure you're correct."

"Well, I still intend to verify your identity."

"Of course."

"In the meantime, if a family reunion isn't your only motivation, you can start by explaining why you're here."

The man's mood sobered. "I am aware Kyle informed you that your father is dead, but what you don't realize are the circumstances around his death."

"He died in a shuttle accident."

"That is only partly true. A bomb destroyed his ship. He was the only passenger and the target of the attack."

"Who the hell would murder him? He wasn't in government and held no political office."

"He was highly regarded and enjoyed a great deal of influence across multiple ministries. After the junta fell, there was a strong movement to elect your father as interim president. That was how he became a target."

"Who was responsible?"

"We're not sure, but the government blamed Thomas."

"What? Kyle told me that bastard died when he was toppled."

"That is the story fed to the public. The reality is that he avoided the roundup of conspirators. He's been in hiding for the past five years, carrying on a reign of terror."

"I'm beginning to understand the nature of the greeting we received."

"Your situation is more dire than you can imagine."

Hayden looked at him askance. "I had nothing to do with Thomas. None of *Scimitar*'s crew did."

"The truth is immaterial. Your fate is already determined, as it is for all your shipmates. You are to be found guilty and publicly executed."

"That is total bullshit. Most of them are civilians, recruited dozens of light years away from here. They have absolutely no involvement with this."

"They only want you and your captain. The others' sentences will be commuted to life imprisonment at the penal colony on Io."

Hayden's shock prevented him from finding the words to express himself. "This is insanity. You're my lawyer. Can't you do something?"

Eli shook his head. "The decision was made at the highest level. You are a double threat to them. If they let you survive, the fear is that your existence will somehow legitimize Thomas's actions and his subsequent claim on power."

"What are you talking about?"

"Thomas was far from universally reviled. The fact is, he is popular enough to allow him to remain well hidden while he wages his insurrection. Letting you live makes things too messy for those in power."

"You said there were two reasons."

"The other revolves around your pedigree. Your father was tagged to take up what was intended for you, not just as interim president, but also as permanent one. As his returned son, generations of your family's machinations paved the way for you to assume that role behind a great deal of influential support."

"I can't believe that to be true. Yes, I was raised with a political agenda in mind, but things are different now. The dreams of my father and his father are meaningless."

"Walden said that you were naive. Trust me when I tell you a lot of very important people breathed a sigh of relief when they heard of your arrival."

"I thought you said you and my father were enemies."

"I never used that word. Despite our differences, I always held immense respect for your father. He reached out to me after you were presumed dead. He wanted to make amends, and I accepted his offer of friendship."

Hayden tried to swallow past his parched throat. "Is Kyle aware of any of this?"

Eli sighed. "No, he believes his case to exonerate you is strong...and before you ask, the only reason I know of the situation is because of my own connections. When I learned of your capture, I volunteered my services to help with your legal defence."

"If I'm a lost cause, why would you do that?"

"Because we are kin, and you are my last connection to my sister...and your father."

"So you thought to take advantage of what little time is available to assuage your guilt at ignoring me all my life?"

Eli snorted derisively. "There are means other than legal that can be applied."

"Huh? Are you talking about..." he lowered his voice to a whisper "... a jailbreak?"

The older man smiled but did not reply.

Hayden scowled. "Why are you taking such a risk for somebody who is practically a stranger? And don't repeat the crap story about us being family. Something is in this for you. What is it?"

Eli stood. "All in due course. Just be ready."

"For what? You didn't tell me a damned thing!"

"You will figure out what you are supposed to do when the time comes. You are not alone in your concern about the approaching menace. There are others who understand that our only hope is in uncovering the secret of the cynosure. You, my lad, and your friends, hold the final piece to that puzzle."

Walk of Destiny

HAYDEN FELT LIKE CRAP.

Sleep had been difficult since his arrest, but after the visit from Eli Gordon, he managed to get none.

Worries for Stella passed through his head during the night instead of dreams. His imagination worked overtime envisioning what she was forced to endure after their ill-considered arrival. Despite her great inner strength, Hayden was aware of her fragility, particularly when overwhelmed by the strong emotions of those around her for long periods.

He hoped her guards, like his, were also synths, and that she was kept as isolated as he. At first he was embarrassed to even entertain that thought, but the more he considered it, the more he wished for it to be true. It was her best chance to conceal the novelty of her empathic ability.

Few empaths survived past their teenage years. Those who did were unstable and spent their lives in psychiatric institutions. If her nature was discovered, she could end her days as a laboratory experiment.

If only they both had the good sense to remain behind at Tau Ceti, they might have enjoyed a few more years together. As things stood, the best outcome she could look forward to was a life of hard labour on Io.

At least until the arrival of the Malliac.

He wondered what fate awaited Cora. She'd probably become somebody's pet science project as they attempted to reverse-engineer the process that bound her to the *Scimitar*.

Pavlovich, too, wandered through his thoughts.

He forced himself to turn away from considering his captain for too long. The emotions the man elicited were hot and cold. He both admired the captain for his uncanny ability to survive impossible odds and resented him for the messes he precipitated.

Hayden considered whether his life would be better if Pavlovich had remained lost somewhere across the galaxy. After consideration, he decided it wouldn't.

If the captain hadn't sought him out, he probably never would have been reunited with Stella or Cora.

Or Pavlovich, for that matter. Despite his conflicted feelings during the restless night, Hayden accepted that he admired him more.

As the synth guards now led him, shackled, through the corridors, he wondered if they might all be tried together. It might be his only opportunity to say goodbye to them before he was taken to his execution.

He had received no recent visits from his uncle or Kyle.

Had the plan that Eli hinted at been uncovered? Perhaps his uncle's implied influence did not run as deep as he believed. The farther he was escorted under armed guard, the more he despaired that they had been found out and now faced their own peril.

Even if they had managed to free him, Eli had mentioned nothing about being able to help his friends.

With every step, his heart grew heavier as he grappled to accept his failure and the inevitability of his death.

With no warning, all four of his android guards stopped.

He looked around, but they were in the middle of a long corridor, with no lifts or doors anywhere nearby.

Each of the synths stood rigid, staring forward, their almost human eyes locked onto something in the distance that he could not see.

A faint peep grabbed his attention, and he searched the air around him for its source.

Seconds later, it sounded again.

And again.

Realizing the sound emanated from his person, he struggled against his shackles to reach into the pocket it seemed to come from.

As he pulled it out, Eli Gordon's holo-business card flashed a bright crimson with the same increasing cadence as the beeping.

The electronic manacles sprang open and fell to the floor.

Confused as to what he was expected to do, he peered down the corridor in both directions.

Deciding that freedom lay in the forward direction, he took tentative steps away from the immobile guards. When they didn't react, he left them behind and ran, checking behind him to see if they had raised their weapons or followed.

He came upon a closed door at the end of the passageway.

Searching about, he could find no way to open it besides the security plate that the synth guard would wave his hand over. With no other idea coming to him, Hayden waved the flashing holo-card in front of the panel, and the lift doors opened.

Once inside, he was faced with his next decision. One button would send the elevator up, presumably toward the courtroom he was intended to arrive at. The downward one, he reasoned, might take him to a garage or mechanical level.

Or it might be the opposite.

Constantly checking down the corridor to see if the guards pursued him, he wrestled with the decision. The last thing he wanted to do was send himself to his own trial.

He examined the card for some indication of what he was expected to do. Finding nothing helpful, he sighed and looked at the lift's control panel.

He waved it over the lower button.

Nothing happened.

He passed it across a second time, with the same result.

Annoyed, he tried the up-going one. The doors slid shut, and the lift began to move.

A few seconds into his journey, panic came over him when he realized he should have taken a gun from one of his guards. Then he reasoned that if he was meant to take one, he would somehow have been given a clue to do so.

He turned the glowing card over, searching for a communication interface. He found only the logo and address of Eli Gordon's legal firm emblazoned on it. Pressing down on it, he hoped it might activate something.

He pressed every letter and symbol on its surface, with no result.

His growing annoyance subsided at the realization of how long the lift had been operating.

Then the elevator's upward movement stopped.

Sweat dripping down his cheek, Hayden stared at the door and tried to prepare himself for anything.

The doors parted, and he was greeted by his uncle.

"What kept you?"

"PUT THESE ON."

Eli shoved boots and folded clothing into Hayden's hands.

"What is—?"

"There is no time. Strip down and get dressed before you delay us any further."

Clamping his lips shut, Hayden stripped off the prison jumpsuit and donned the guard's uniform while his rescuer kept a lookout.

They were in an air-car hangar, and while nobody was around, it was apparent from the number of expensive, neatly parked vehicles that they would not remain unseen for long.

"These boots are too small."

"Make it work. You only have to look the part until we clear the security gates."

As Hayden struggled with the ill-fitting footwear, Eli stuffed the discarded garment and slippers into his briefcase.

With Hayden's toes scrunched painfully, he could only get the fasteners partly closed. "That is the best I can do."

Eli studied Hayden's feet for a second, frowning. "It'll do. C'mon, we're losing our time window."

He strode ahead, forcing Hayden to catch up with him. "What is the plan?"

Eli checked his wrist chronometer. "Walk now. Talk later," he said and doubled his pace.

Hayden ignored the pain in his feet and matched his uncle's stride.

They came upon a nervous-looking Kyle standing beside a limousine waiting in a passenger zone.

"Where were you?"

"We're here now." Eli turned to address Hayden. "Can you operate a vehicle?"

"Yes, but—"

As he spoke, the driver got out and stood next to Kyle. Hayden swore the man was his own twin.

"Who is that?"

Kyle plucked the cap from the man's head and pushed it into Hayden's hands. "Shut up and get in before you're seen. The surveillance cameras won't be off for much longer."

As Hayden settled into the driver's seat, he watched in open-mouthed fascination as the face of its former occupant seemed to waver and then resolve into somebody completely different.

Eli handed the briefcase to Kyle. "You need to move, you're almost late."

He passed the case to the other man, who walked back in the direction Hayden and his uncle came from.

When Eli had seated himself into the passenger compartment, Kyle leaned into the still opened door. "I warned you about the timing."

"We are still within the window, but you must be in that courtroom before the alarm sounds."

"And you two have to be outside of the compound gates. Get moving." He closed the door and banged on the roof to signal them to go.

Taking his cue, Hayden activated the a-gravs, and the vehicle rose from the deck and moved forward along the only way they could proceed.

"What are we going to do when we get to the security check?" he said over his shoulder. "This disguise isn't going to fool anyone for very long."

"It only needs to get us through the gate. You look like the driver who brought me here, and that is all they will see unless we're caught inside when the alarm goes off. Then we will be screwed, so you should hurry us along without appearing to be in a rush."

Hayden accelerated them to as fast as he dared go until he had to slow down on approach to the gate.

"Keep your eyes focused forward," said Eli. "And try not to appear so nervous. Everything is going according to plan."

They floated up to the guard station, and he rolled down both his window and Eli's at the direction of the officer. The soldier didn't pay attention to Hayden and instead addressed his uncle.

"Only a short visit today, Mister Gordon?"

"My client found a way to put himself into the infirmary overnight. I'll return when his jaw is no longer wired shut and we can carry on an intelligent conversation."

The guard chuckled as he straightened. He took another, more careful check of Hayden before he signalled for the gate to be opened. They were a kilometre away from the facility and pulling onto the aeroway when Hayden finally allowed himself to relax and breathe normally.

"I think we've made it," said Eli. "I was worried you took a gun from one of your guards. That would have complicated matters."

"It would have helped if you gave me some instructions."

He caught Eli's growing smile in the rear viewer. "You made out fine without them, but I take your point. That was my oversight. I should have instructed you on how to access them on the card. In my defence, this is my first jailbreak."

"What is going to happen to Kyle and your other man?"

"If he arrived at the courtroom before your absence is discovered, he will be fine. As for my associate, well, he has more experience in such matters."

"Do your associates make a habit of getting people out of that place?"

"Not that particular facility."

"What kind of a law practice do you run, anyway?"

"I specialize in fixing problems. I must admit, your case is more challenging than most."

After proceeding for another minute, Hayden asked, "So where are we going?"

"Oh, sorry. Activate program number six, then you can relax and take off those shoes if they still hurt you."

When his toes stopped cramping, he turned in his seat to face his rescuer. "What happened back there? The guards just halted in their tracks and went dormant or something."

"You can thank that card in your pocket. It emitted a signal to the synths that shut them down for about twenty minutes."

"Won't they sound the alarm when they wake up and discover me gone?"

"No, because we accessed their core controllers. The reset sent them back in time. They returned to your cell to extract you, giving us the additional time we needed to get out of the facility. Had you taken one of their weapons, however, different protocols would have activated, and we likely wouldn't be having this conversation."

"You and Kyle were my only visitors. Won't suspicion fall on you?"

"As I said, he is safe as long as he was waiting for you in the courtroom when you were reported missing. He'll be questioned, but he's been coached, and, of course, kept ignorant of critical details."

"And you? After all, the guard saw you leaving with me."

Eli smiled. "He saw me depart with the same driver I arrived with. That, and a little security recording error, courtesy of that marvellous little card in your possession, should cover my tracks perfectly."

"How did you get your hands on this tech? That holo-masque was far more complex than the commercial ones in costume shops."

"You'll meet the creator of those gadgets after we get you to safety." Eli paused. "Excuse me, I'm receiving an urgent message on my LINK."

Hayden turned his attention to the view while his uncle took the call. He wasn't told what city they were in, so he searched for any familiar landmarks on the ground, two thousand metres below them.

When it was clear Eli was finished, he said, "I don't recognize where we are."

"Just outside of Kiev. I just received word that Stella is waiting for us at the safe house."

"Oh, thank God, you got her out. Were you able to spring Pavlovich too?"

Frowning, Eli hesitated before responding. "That was impossible."

"No! They'll execute him. He has to be freed as well."

"I'm sorry, Hayden, it can't be done right now."

"Why the hell not? You broke me out of a maximum-security military facility. How much harder could it be to get him out of one too?"

"First, we can't use the same tactic, but tactics are not our problem."

"Well, what is?"

"Pavlovich is missing."

Confessions

"THANK GOODNESS YOU'RE all right!"

Hayden had just gotten through the door to the safe house when Stella threw herself into his arms, pulling him close. They embraced tightly for several seconds before he heard a throat clearing.

Separating, they both faced Eli, who wore a smile.

"Stella, this is my uncle."

"Yes, we've met. He got me released."

"Oh, right. He told me that." He frowned at Eli. "But he has yet to spring Pavlovich."

"I told you, nothing can be done."

"Well, it sounds to me like you won't even bother trying."

"Pavlovich's situation is far more complicated than you can possibly imagine. He's not on Earth."

"Do you know where he is?" asked Stella.

"The information I received during the journey here is conflicting. I instructed my associates to suss out the truth, but it will take time."

"The truth about what?" said Hayden.

The older man grew silent, appearing to weigh the wisdom of telling them more. Finally, he said, "He *was* with your ship at the orbital defence platform."

"What do you mean 'was?' Where is he now?"

Eli shook his head. "Nobody knows. A short time ago, a well-trained attack force boarded the facility and made off with Pavlovich...and the *Scimitar*. The damage was significant. The military is doing everything in its power to cover things up and spin the event as a war games accident, but in the meantime planetary security is tighter than usual. By dumb luck, your escape happened at about the same time and is being considered as related. Kyle is being detained pending a full investigation."

"That's terrible," said Stella.

"I made sure he knew as little as possible about the operation for his own protection. If he plays his part properly, he should be freed soon."

"Is there anything you can do for him?"

"I dare not for fear of making his situation more precarious. I trust in his ability to follow the plan."

"I hope so," said Hayden. "The last thing I wanted was for him to come to harm helping me."

"It was his free choice to do so, as it is mine," said Eli. "As things stand, we should turn our attention to other pressing matters, such as the cynosure."

"How does he know about that?" she said to Hayden.

"A good question," he said, looking at his uncle.

Eli shook his head and sat in a chair. "I should have listened to my mother."

"About what?"

"Your grandmother used to tell me when I was a boy that even the smallest deception is a net in which we can easily become entangled."

"You're not making any sense."

He smiled weakly. "Stella, I understand that you are an empath. Can you determine if a person is telling a lie?"

Her brow furrowed. "Not always, but often. Why?"

"I want you to read me to verify what I am about to say is truthful."

"Why do you need her to do that?"

Eli sighed. "Up to this moment, I have been telling you half-truths—basically lying to you—about certain facts. I want to come clean and give you the entire story, but..." He shrugged.

"By admitting that, you've sown the seed for mistrust in anything you say from this point on," said Hayden.

"If Stella can verify the truth of what I next tell you, it will set the record straight and go toward repairing the damage to our relationship."

"Unless you are a brilliant liar and fool me," she said. "You are a lawyer, after all."

He laughed. "Too true. Will you at least accept my word that I am sincere?"

She stared at him. Finally, she shrugged. "He is, as far as I can tell."

She sat down in another chair, leaving Hayden the only one standing. He crossed his arms and turned to Eli. "Okay, I'm listening."

"First, a full disclosure of what happened in the government, then my respective role and association."

He nodded. "Fine."

"To begin, everything I told you about how Thomas seized control was true. What I did not explain was his motivation. When those in power received your warning prior to the gate collapse, almost nobody took it seriously."

"But some did," said Hayden.

"Yes, chief among them was Admiral Robert Thomas. He was the presidential military advisor. He argued vigorously for the president and the executive council to heed the message, but they laughed him out of the meeting."

"Wait a minute, how do you know all of this?"

A wan smile formed on Eli's lips. "My role in events will become clear soon enough, but I was there. I was a member of the inner cabinet; attorney general, to be precise."

Hayden's eyes widened, and he turned to Stella, his unspoken question written on his face.

"As far as I can tell, he's being truthful," she said.

Hayden nodded for Eli to continue.

"When the light gate network collapsed—as you warned us it would—against my advice the administration declared martial law. Civil rights were curtailed, curfews imposed, and thousands of people arrested; conveniently, most were political opponents. I resigned in protest, but it did nothing to rein in the excess. I believed that others would follow my lead, and President Merrimac would be forced to end martial law."

"But things got worse?" said Stella.

Eli nodded sadly. "Instead of heeding Thomas's warning that the network collapse was proof the Confederacy was under threat, the president and his council argued that order had to be maintained. A police state was the result."

"Where were you and my father in all this?"

"On the sidelines; I did my best to work within the restrictive legal system to find justice for as many as I could, but my efforts, sadly, did not make a great difference. Walden was affected by the events. Everything your family had worked for over generations was collapsing around him. When it became clear you were forever lost to him and probably dead, he buried himself in trying to maintain and reconstruct whatever connections he could, hopeful things might turn around. With all the purging of government departments, it was a hopeless effort. "

"Why were neither of you tagged as a dissenter?"

Eli shrugged. "We were viewed as toothless old lions. I think they believed allowing me to defend their victims in the courts somehow legitimized the facade that they still respected the rule of law. Your father assisted me when he could, but we were pissing on a forest fire."

"What about Thomas?"

"He became a more vocal opponent as popular unrest rose. Fanning the flames made him a target of the police. They branded him a political dissident and enemy of the state and forced him into hiding."

Eli grew quiet and fought to control tears. "Please forgive me, but I lost a number of friends in those days."

"Of course," said Stella, her own eyes glistening. "Take your time."

He sniffled. "I'm all right."

He straightened his back and cleared his throat. "About a year or so after his disappearance, Thomas paid me a clandestine visit. He confided in me that he was preparing a coup and wanted my support. I must admit, I was disillusioned enough that I listened to him. His pitch was a lot of political posturing and the typical promises one might expect, but then he mentioned something different and revealed his greatest motivation for fostering a revolution. He called it the cynosure, an ancient alien technology uncovered in an archaeological dig over a century ago."

"We are familiar with it," said Hayden. "The Glenatat disassembled the device and scattered the components throughout their empire before it collapsed. We've spent the past year locating the last pieces."

"How did you learn of it?" asked Eli.

"From Pavlovich; Thomas told him about it when he tried to recruit him to some kind of shadow group with the intent to topple the government."

"Eh? This is news to me. How long ago did this happen?"

"I'm not sure. It was a few years before the collapse. He was reassigned to the frontier systems because of his refusal to help Thomas."

Eli nodded. "Interesting—and typical; Robert did not take rejection well, though it is disturbing to learn he'd planned a coup years earlier than I'd believed."

"The coup was obviously a success," said Stella.

"Yes, but it generated a lot of political waves. Various factions that supported him took exception to Thomas's agenda once he gained power. He was an ardent believer that the Confederacy was in danger from an 'overwhelming threat,' as he used to call it. He poured billions of credits into technological research that others believed should have gone toward reconstruction. Many refused to believe him, branding him as the architect of events as a justification for him to seize power."

"Dad was one of his opponents?"

"I'm afraid so. He worked behind the scenes to oust Thomas."

"And in revenge was murdered by him."

Eli sighed. "Robert was blamed, yes..."

"You don't believe he was behind it?" said Stella.

"It is difficult for me to accept the idea that one of my friends could murder another one."

"They were not friends," said Hayden angrily. "Thomas as much as told me himself before he sent me to *Scimitar*."

"But they were both mine, and that is what I struggle with."

"Do you believe it is possible that he murdered my father?"

"I admit that Robert is certainly capable of doing it. But whether he actually would is another question."

"Why are you telling us all of this?" said Hayden.

"This is the part you are not going to like," said Eli. "The attack on the orbital defence platform was orchestrated by Thomas. He did it to obtain the last components of the cynosure device."

"Do you know where he is?"

He looked at them sadly. "I promised you both that I would be truthful. The answer is yes."

"Then you are going to take us to him," said Hayden.

Rendezvous

THE HOLO-MASQUE EMITTER chaffed Hayden's neck beneath his collar. Despite Eli's assurances that it worked perfectly, he felt exposed as they walked from the car to the private hangar.

Stella seemed to be more at ease wearing hers, which enfolded her face with a convincing stranger's visage. Even under scrutiny in the air-car, he could not detect any flaw that might give her away.

Still, despite the evidence and assurances, he was nervous as he handed his forged ID to the soldier monitoring the entrance. The guard and his companion looked bored and did not pay more than a cursory glance to any of their party before granting them admission.

Without delay, they were ushered to a drop ship waiting to carry them to a pleasure yacht parked in orbit.

Once Eli finished his conversation with their pilot, he joined Hayden and Stella in the passenger compartment.

"You can turn off you masks now," he told them.

Hayden took little time to deactivate and remove the device.

"Don't scratch," said Stella. "You're leaving a mark on your neck."

"Was yours not itchy? I wanted to claw my skin off."

"I think you were just anxious," she said, smiling.

"I'd make a lousy spy if I had to wear one of those things a lot." He rubbed his neck but stopped upon remembering Stella's warning.

"More foolproof methods of concealment are used in espionage circles," said Eli.

"How is it you know that?" asked Stella.

He flashed her a disarming smile. "My clientele is diverse."

"Who is Arthur Slocam?" said Hayden, scrutinizing the identification he carried.

"He and his wife, Clarissa, are my good friends. They are on an extended business trip to Callisto. He grants me free use of his yacht when he is not using it."

"I was surprised by how casual those soldiers were. With the high-security alert, I expected a pat-down or a detailed scan."

"They are well compensated to look the other way."

"What kind of business does your friend run?" asked Stella.

"None that we need concern ourselves with."

The drop ship's engine whine rose in pitch, and Hayden was sucked into the luxurious upholstery. He gazed out the port, grateful for a glimpse of the receding blue planet.

When the artificial gravity kicked in and the view out the window changed to the black of space, he turned to Eli.

"Where are we headed?"

"We will rendezvous with the *Rio Grande* and then follow the commercial spacing lanes until we pass Luna. From there, we will deactivate our transponder and proceed to the designated coordinates."

"Who is meeting us?"

"I don't know," said Eli. "Nor can I anticipate the kind of reception we will receive when we arrive. This trip breaks almost every contact protocol Thomas put in place."

"Is there a danger we will be fired on?" asked Stella.

"The odds are overwhelming that will happen. My signal codes may be out of date. I warned you that this was risky."

"There is no time to play it safe."

Eli grunted and peered out his window. "That is the only reason I agreed to this."

· · · ·

Fourteen hours later, the yacht waited at the meeting coordinates for a response to their signal.

Too nervous to remain seated, Hayden rose. He felt Eli's eyes follow him as he paced about the cabin.

"Are you usually this anxious?"

"On *Scimitar* we didn't make a habit of hanging around and waiting for somebody to come by and shoot at us."

"Yes," said Eli, "you're probably used to having something with which to shoot back."

Hayden stopped and looked at him. "You're not really helping."

"Sorry. Would you feel better if I joined you in your anxiety?"

"No. Why aren't you worried, if you believe your codes might be outdated?"

"Years in the courtroom taught me to hide it, but I'm nervous. Aren't I, Stella?"

She looked from Eli to Hayden. "The two of you are starting to get to me."

"There, we're giving the young woman anxiety as well. I'm sorry, my dear, I'm sure we both can manage to find our courage for a short time."

The lighting dimmed to an electric blue glow. The captain's shaky voice came over the speaker. "Mister Gordon, we've been hailed."

"Did you send the code sequence I gave you?"

"Yes, sir, but their missile ports have opened. How do you wish me to proceed?"

"Repeat it. Tell them I am aboard the ship, and the son of Walden Kaine is with me."

The intercom clicked off.

"Why did you tell them about me?"

"To be honest, I couldn't think of anything else to tell them."

"Sir," said the captain, now sounding more confident, "we've been ordered to shut down our drive and rig to be towed."

"You may comply," Eli told him. Turning to Hayden, he said, "It appears I guessed correctly about Thomas being interested in you."

"Yeah," said Hayden, "now we only have to find out if that is good or bad."

· · · ·

Another three hours passed as the mystery vessel took the *Rio* under tow. With nothing to see out the window, it seemed like the ship was not moving. The absence of vibrations from the drive engine made for silence, which only compounded Hayden's unease.

"Honestly," said Eli, "I'm not an empath, and I can sense your anxiety. Stella has been patient with you, but I am sure you are fraying her nerves as well. Try to relax."

"That is easier said than done. The last time I spoke with Thomas, he was assigning me to the *Scimitar* to get me as far from Earth as possible."

"Why would he do that?"

Hayden's cheeks grew warm as he considered Stella. "He did not want me near his granddaughter."

Eli nodded. "Robert is very protective of that remarkable young woman. I trust you and she parted on good terms?"

"Not exactly."

"I see. That is unfortunate, but perhaps enough time has passed to heal the rift."

"Either that or he wants to finish what the Malliac didn't."

He glanced at Stella, who sat rigid with her arms crossed and a pissed-off look on her face.

Eli chuckled. "At least you aren't sharing your nerves with poor Stella anymore."

"Would you two please just shut up?" she said then turned to gaze out the window.

Hayden had long before shared with her his history with Katherine Myers-Thomas. They had been an item throughout Hayden's years as a cadet, having met during his first term. Katie, though only a year ahead of him, was set to graduate at the end of his first term. To say she was brilliant was like referring to the sun as just a light in the sky. She graduated with the commensurate rank of captain and was promptly assigned to the UEF weapons research lab. She quickly rose, and by the time Hayden neared graduation, a staff of a dozen worked under her.

Robert Thomas was exceedingly proud of his only grandchild and very protective of her.

In any other relationship, Stella's cold treatment would be an irrational and without justifiable merit. Her empathic ability, however, made things far more difficult. He could not conceal his automatic reaction to the mention of Katie. The prospect that they might somehow meet again, no matter how remote or improbable, had excited him for a fraction of a second. Nobody but Stella would know that happened.

He thought his years spent on the other side of the galactic arm had smothered his feelings for Katie, and he'd assured Stella that was the case long ago. Now, a tiny, unguarded emotion had thrown up an obstacle between them that should not be there, and it made him sick.

Stella was a rational woman, brilliant in her own right. She had no cause for worry or jealousy, and he wanted to sidle up next to her to cajole and reassure her she need not be concerned. It would be the proper thing for him to do.

But he couldn't.

She would see right through him that the embers of that old relationship were not extinguished, and there remained the potential for them to be fanned to life.

It was nothing he would consciously do. They had lived together for over a decade, grown closer, and experienced more growth than he and Katie ever had.

His relationship with Katie had been hormonal, nothing more. Why could Stella not understand that?

Or perhaps she did and needed some time to come to terms with having to compete for him with a ghost he might never encounter.

Hayden almost laughed aloud over how foolish he was.

Guilty, he looked toward Stella, who gazed back, a wry smile on her pretty face.

Grinning, he sat beside her and enveloped her in a tight embrace. "I would never hurt you," he whispered. "I love you."

"I love you too, and I can't be angry with you over something you didn't do. Please forgive me?"

Eli cleared his throat loudly. "We seem to be at our destination."

Hayden and Stella both hurried to the other side of the ship to look out the window.

Slowly growing larger as they approached was a massive asteroid. He could just make out the camouflaged cowlings for the defensive weapons array that dotted its surface. Moored to the rock were three warships.

One of them was *Scimitar*.

Reunions

THE *Rio Grande* connected to a retractable docking causeway leading inside the base. Similar structures ran likewise to the other ships, making the asteroid look like half of a spider.

Upon exiting the tunnel, Hayden deactivated his magnetic boots as he felt the transition to artificial gravity. The narthex they stood in was carved out of the rock, and numerous tunnels led away from the chamber into the warren that was Thomas's base.

Waiting for him, white teeth peeking out from under his bushy beard, was a familiar smiling face.

"Pavlovich!" Hayden never imagined himself being so happy to see the man. He hurried forward, arm extended to shake his captain's hand.

Pavlovich ignored it and pulled him into a bear hug.

"I'm glad you're here," he said before he released Hayden and enveloped Stella in a similar embrace. She endured the unrestrained affection before relenting and returning the hug.

"I'm happy you are both safe," he said as they disengaged.

He stopped to consider Eli, who smiled and extended his hand.

"I'm Eli Gordon, Hayden's uncle."

The captain's grin returned as they shook hands. "Of course, I've heard a great deal about you. Thanks for your help in springing these two."

He turned to give Hayden the once-over. "The last I saw of you, your face was being ground into the deck plating. I'm sure Stella is glad they didn't damage that pretty face. Where'd they take you?"

"Eli helped me escape from the military detention complex in Kiev."

"Wow, that was some accomplishment." Pavlovich regarded Stella. "And how about you, young lady? What tower were you plucked from?"

She scowled and was about to reply when Eli interrupted. "Is Robert here yet?"

"Yeah. He hasn't left *Scimitar* since she docked. I swear, if Cora still had an ass, his nose would be buried up it. He can't learn about our modifications fast enough and is starting to make a pest of himself."

"Did she actually tell you that?" asked Stella.

"Not in so many words."

"I need to speak with him," said Eli.

"Follow me, everyone." Pavlovich started toward one of the tunnels, and Hayden fell into step beside him.

"How about you?" he asked the captain. "What happened?"

"They hustled me off, hog-tied, just like you. I was taken to Marlene's command ship, but she treated me decently. She apologized all over the place about having to follow orders and confined me to a cabin. I got three squares a day but was kept isolated. I never even saw her after that. Once we got to the orbital platform, the party was over, and I was thrown into a windowless cell the size of the head in my quarters on *Scimitar*."

"I had a similar experience, minus the guest cabin."

"The brig, eh? Your first time, I'll bet."

"It wasn't a highlight of the past few days. What happened after you arrived?"

"Things got a bit testy; lots of interrogation, not much sleeping. No torture, but I got the impression they considered it."

"What did they want?"

"They were convinced I knew where Thomas was hiding. For some reason, they believed we've been working under his orders for the last decade."

"That's the story I got too. They never even questioned me about anything, just decided I was guilty of high treason and not worthy of a trial. I was being led off for sentencing when Eli busted me out."

"I'm not sure what they next had planned for me," said Pavlovich, "but they were interrupted when Thomas's troops raided the base. They grabbed me and *Scimitar* and brought us here."

"What about the rest of the crew?"

"I can't find out where any of them are being held, but Thomas promised to get them freed."

"You believe him?"

Pavlovich turned to regard Hayden, one eyebrow raised. "Your only experience of him is as the head of the academy. He cultivated his reputation in that place over a lot of years, but the man himself is not quite the same martinet you knew. Don't get me wrong, he is still a prick, but he treats everyone I know with the same respect."

"You are singing a different tune about him."

"What can I say? I owe him my freedom, if not my life. I'm compelled out of gratitude to look for some redeeming qualities in the man."

Hayden was smiling at the comment when they exited the tunnel into another chamber.

The entrance to the causeway leading to *Scimitar* was abuzz with activity. Technicians were coming and going in a manner that reminded him of a beehive.

"What the hell are they doing to her?"

"I told you, Thomas wants to learn about all the Glenatat modifications. Every available specialist of his is working on this."

"And you're okay with this?"

"We all share the same goal, so yes."

As he spoke, a trim-looking man in his late seventies stepped from *Scimitar*. His close haircut and familiar scowl confirmed his identity to Hayden instantly.

"Robert, there you are," said Eli as he broke away from the group and went to greet his friend. The two men shared an enthusiastic back-patting greeting. Pavlovich winked and led them to meet Thomas.

As they walked toward him, the only thing that Hayden could think of was his dead father and the fact that he was about to confront the man accused of the murder.

The admiral caught sight of them approaching and turned his attention toward them. "Mister Kaine, you're a person I never thought to see again."

He swallowed the lump in his throat and bit back a reply. Recalling their last meeting, he was unsure how to take Thomas's comment. Then the older man removed all doubt when his frown dissolved into a fatherly smile and he extended a hand.

Fighting his rising anger, Hayden accepted it, and they shook. "I guess I'm hard to get rid of, sir."

Thomas did not seem to detect the undertone of Hayden's reply. "Something I'm grateful for. We all owe you a great debt of gratitude. Your courageous decision to take down the network gave humanity time to prepare for the approaching storm."

"Our chances are better if we can access the cynosure," interjected Pavlovich.

"Plans are already in motion to that end. Which reminds me, I'd like the both of you at the strategy meeting at 09:40."

"I want Miss Gabriel to attend as well," said Pavlovich as he stepped aside to introduce her.

The admiral shook Stella's hand. "It is a pleasure to meet you. Please accept my sincere condolences for the loss of your father. If not for his work, I can't imagine how bad our situation might be."

"Thank you. I too wish he could be here."

"Naturally, your experience with the Malliac is invaluable, and I would appreciate your insights at our meeting."

"I am pleased to be able to help where I can."

"You're far too modest, Doctor Gabriel." Thomas turned to address the rest of them. "I shall see you all there. In the meantime, Eli and I have matters to discuss. Please feel free to inspect your ship in the interim. I suspect my people have a hundred questions for you."

With that, he excused himself and went off down a tunnel with Hayden's uncle.

Hayden turned to Stella. "Doctor Gabriel?"

"I hold the equivalent of two doctorate degrees. You knew that."

"Yeah, but I didn't think he did. How much did you tell him about us, Pavlovich?"

"He's been over our logs a dozen times. I think he is familiar with everything about us at this point."

"He didn't seem to be aware that we left Stella's father on the Glenatat homeward."

"Oh?" said the captain as he walked to the causeway. "That must not have made it into my log." They followed him aboard *Scimitar*.

As Hayden stood just inside the ship, watching the small army of researchers and engineers bustle about, a familiar voice called out to him from behind.

Heart in his throat, he turned to see the beautiful face of Katie Meyers-Thomas.

Old Flames

"KATIE!" SAID HAYDEN, his voice almost cracking.

Despite hoping he might encounter her at some point, he was not prepared to find her aboard *Scimitar*. Butterflies that hadn't had wings in years flew chaotically in his stomach as he searched for words that would not come.

"I'm so glad you're alive," she said as she rushed to him and pulled him into a tight embrace.

Hayden was unsure how to respond to the unexpected show of affection and patted her on the back. He cleared his throat and looked over to Stella.

Katie blushed and stepped back a couple of paces.

"Katie, this is Stella, my..." His mind went blank over how to define their relationship.

She leaned forward to shake Katie's hand. "We've been together for almost ten years." She shot Hayden a glance that told him he was going to pay later.

"Oh." Katie's blush deepened. "Of course." Seeming also to have lost the capacity for speech, she accepted and shook Stella's hand.

The pecking order established, their demeanour changed, with Stella growing more confident and Katie more distant.

Pavlovich cleared his throat. "We've already met."

Attempting to break the awkward tension, Hayden said, "What do you think of *Scimitar*?"

Katie's eyes widened and her face lit up, her embarrassment now apparently forgotten. "She's amazing! I can't believe the technology...and your engineer, Cora; she's brilliant and has been so helpful."

He smiled. If she was going to bond with anyone, it would be Cora. "We wouldn't be here if not for her."

"And the machine she's melded to is fascinating. I'd love to study how much her intellect is enhanced by the alien AI she's merged with."

Hayden frowned at the idea of Cora being viewed more as a lab specimen than a person. "You should visit her in her VR, if she invites you. You'll understand her a lot better that way."

"What are all these people doing on *Scimitar*?" asked Stella, clearly trying to change the subject.

Katie's expression changed to the serious one Hayden had always called "work mode." "We got an initial look at some of the Glenatat technology from the transport ship that brought your messengers back ten years ago. While its hull gave us some information for our metallurgical research, its interfaces were surprisingly primitive."

"They were adapted for humans to pilot them," said Hayden.

She nodded. "When we learned of the adaptations to *Scimitar* and her dark energy weapon, however, it was like striking the motherlode. This ship is a godsend, given the alien threat."

"Not to mention her FTL drive," said Pavlovich like a proud parent.

"Yes, the science behind it is very interesting and will change our understanding of physics."

"Of course, but I was referring to what it can do to reconnect the Confederation."

Katie shook her head. "After my discussions with Cora, we agree that it is flawed and too dangerous at this stage. Perhaps after more research, though..."

"Now just a minute," said the captain, "just because there are a few bugs to be worked out doesn't mean the technology is useless. It transported us around the galaxy quite well, thank you."

"Yes, I realize that," she said, an edge of annoyance in her voice, "but there is still a significant flaw that makes it impractical. How is your cancer, by the way?"

The air grew icy as Pavlovich scowled at her. "I was treated. I'm fine."

"You were lucky," said Katie. "While the FTL drive may yet prove usable, the missing components for the cynosure device you brought are *Scimitar*'s most valuable treasure. "

"You're aware of it?" said Stella.

Katie raised a condescending eyebrow at her. "My grandfather took me into his confidence. I spent many years assembling and studying it and probably understand more about it than anyone alive."

"You have access to the device?" said Hayden. "Is it here?"

"Ah, no." Her arrogance was suddenly gone.

"Where is it?" asked Pavlovich.

"It was in a special laboratory at the Lunar Military Research Institute."

"Where is it *now*?" asked Stella.

"I... I don't know. It was moved after Grandfather was deposed."

"Well, that doesn't do us much good, does it?" said Pavlovich.

"My grandfather's agents turned up a significant lead as to its whereabouts."

"A lead?" said Stella.

Katie's pretty face contorted into a scowl. "He's doing the best he can."

"That may not be good enough. I hope you learned a lot from *Scimitar*. You're going to need advanced manufacturing capacity lined up to refit your ships with armour and weapons to defend against the approaching Malliac horde."

Katie seemed stunned, as if she'd never been spoken to like that before. As Hayden thought about it, he realized she probably hadn't.

"Okay, ladies," said Pavlovich, smirking. "As much as I want to see which of you would come out on top in an all-out catfight..."

Both women glared at him.

His smile growing, he continued. "We may have some information about the cynosure device's location. Thomas called us all to a meeting on this very topic."

Without another word, he and Katie turned and headed for the access hatch. Stella and Hayden followed them from the ship and down the tunnel, slowing their pace to put some distance between the pair, who were engrossed in an animated conversation.

He smiled at how Pavlovich seemed to take cruel pleasure in pushing Katie's hot buttons.

"I don't understand what you ever saw in her," said Stella.

"I told you before; I was young, and it was a hormonal attraction." He wanted to add that Katie was also gorgeous, but he wasn't suicidal.

Continuing as if she hadn't heard him, she said, "I don't care how clever she's supposed to be. She's arrogant, condescending—"

"I think you're just as brilliant."

She glared at him. "Stop trying to mollify me."

"Cora too."

Stella stared at him, but her frown twitched as her anger dissipated. "You really think we're just as brilliant as your old flame?"

"Absolutely. I've known you twice as long as I knew her. I can attest to it under oath. In fact..."

She put her arms around his waist. "Shut up, Kaine. You're off the hook."

"Well, I'm relieved. I'm not sure where I would sleep tonight, otherwise."

She punched him playfully on the arm. "Asshole."

"Hey, you two," called Pavlovich from ahead. "You can snog later. We've got a civilization to save."

They smiled at each other, then continued, hand in hand.

HAYDEN CONSIDERED THE people in the room.

The base's mess hall had been commandeered, and several tables were pushed together for everyone to sit around.

Stella and Pavlovich sat on either side of him, while Eli, Katie, and Thomas all occupied chairs across from them, from where they ran the meeting. In the remaining ten seats were various technical and military specialists Hayden met before the gathering was called to order.

A surprising late arrival was Kyle. He seemed collected for a man recently held under suspicion of engineering Hayden's escape. Hayden wondered how difficult a time his friend had experienced on his behalf and whether Eli was responsible for another jailbreak. He offered Hayden a curt nod before sitting next to his mentor, with whom he now shared a hushed discussion.

Disturbed by his manner, Hayden nudged Stella and indicated Kyle.

"What's wrong?" she whispered.

"He's tense."

"He just got out of custody."

"Maybe, but something seems off with him."

"I don't sense anything unusual. Why don't you leave the empath stuff to me and focus on the meeting?"

He squeezed her hand and turned his attention to what Thomas was saying.

"...confirmed the location of the cynosure device. It was transported to the Titan armoury."

A low buzz of voices filled the room as the significance of the situation was realized. Thomas called for order.

"It is common knowledge how formidable the defences around the station are. Let's not get caught up in that and lose sight of our purpose. You've all been briefed about what our objective is. You also are aware of what we achieved in liberating *Scimitar*. That was no mean feat. Titan will require more planning." A grim smile turned up the corners of his mouth, as if he savoured the challenge. He then indicated for Kyle to take up the briefing.

As his former schoolmate stood and straightened his jacket, Hayden saw how much his old roommate had matured. Where once he might have only seen a fellow cadet with far more ambition than skill or wisdom, Kyle now was a seasoned leader. A better student than himself; more than once, Kyle's notes had saved Hayden from his lax attendance to his studies. But he always seemed to be held back by something, routinely deferring to Hayden's own brash impulsiveness, which got them both into trouble. Now there was a confidence behind the warm brown eyes that was not there before. He realized his friend had developed a taste for ambition and had the ability to realize it.

"My recent sojourn as a guest of the military courts provided me an opportunity to speak with some of my contacts," said Kyle. "While they spoke from different perspectives, the underlying message I received was the same. The government's resources are spread thin. Our attack on the orbital platform prompted the redeployment of ships and personnel to protect facilities identified as potential targets. Every indication is that Titan is absent from that list."

"Why is that?" asked one of the tacticians at the table. "It is the key military installation in the system."

"And much too far removed," said Thomas. "All of our disruptive activity has been deliberately directed at Earth and Luna. As far as High Command is concerned, the facility is too difficult for us to consider it a viable target to make a political statement."

"And therein lies the means to how we will gain access," said Kyle. He waved an arm to activate the holographic projector in the middle of the room and strode toward the image. The spherical orbital facility floated menacingly above the featureless orange moon.

"The outer system defences are coordinated from Titan base." Another wave of his hand, and the hologram zoomed to a false-coloured portion of the moon's surface. It morphed to reveal a schematic plan of a facility. "The Cassini armoury is subterranean, located ten kilometres underground inside a dormant cryovolcano."

"The atmospheric conditions and depth of burial are its only ground defences," said Pavlovich.

"That, and a single access point," said Thomas, "and, of course, we must get past the orbital base. It possesses enough firepower to wipe out whatever direct assault we might be able to mount."

"Which is why that is not the tactic we will employ," said Kyle with a conspiratorial smile. "At least with that intention in mind."

Thomas stood and waved his arm to return the image to a view from outside of Titan's orbit. A small armada appeared on approach to the moon.

"We will act as they do not suspect we dare," said the admiral. "A task force will make an overt run at the defence facility."

"They'll see it coming," said Pavlovich, rising. "Those ships won't get close before they're intercepted and cut to pieces by the warships based there."

Thomas smiled. "They won't be in a position to do that. They will be addressing an incursion near the light gate."

"What sort of incursion?"

"The facility is on high alert, watching for any sign of the Malliac threat."

"I thought the current government doesn't take that seriously," said Hayden.

"They don't," said Thomas, "but the military does. Since your warning, Mister Kaine, Titan's long-range monitoring system has been watching for signs of them."

"That's why they were so quick to notice us when we arrived," said Pavlovich.

"It is also why they will spot you again."

"You're going to use *Scimitar* to draw them out? That may distract a few ships, but what they keep behind and the facility's rail gun will still make short shrift of your fleet."

"Why don't you allow us to finish telling you the plan before you start shitting on it, Captain?"

Pavlovich scowled and sat.

Kyle continued with the briefing. "*Scimitar* will use its FTL drive to jump to the light gate location. There it will deploy its drones, modified to emit signals imitating Malliac dark matter ships."

"You can detect them?" asked Hayden.

"With the information you sent us a decade ago, our researchers developed a way to see them," said Katie. "Our technology is not as advanced as what is aboard *Scimitar*, but it is still effective."

"They'll throw everything they have at us," said Pavlovich.

"That is the response plan in place," said Thomas.

"That still leaves the base rail gun. You won't get near Titan."

"They aren't intended to," said Kyle. "Once the fleet deploys to engage the perceived Malliac incursion, our ships will emerge from their concealed locations within the asteroid belt and approach on high burn. We will also be incorporating drones to send out signals, making the task force appear larger than it is."

"The two events will throw the defensive AI into confusion," said Thomas, "which is all the distraction we'll need."

"Need for what?" said the captain.

"*Scimitar* will use the FTL drive to jump into Titan's atmosphere while the defence systems are otherwise engaged."

"Are you out of your mind?" said Pavlovich. "We can't target our arrival location that finely. We could end up inside the moon."

"We can improve the level of precision," said Katie. "Cora and I are in agreement that it is possible."

"But is it advisable?" said Stella. "You're aware of the effects of the technology on humans, and on *Scimitar*'s structure. Two consecutive jumps like that may destroy the ship or kill her crew."

"We came up with a way to mitigate the distortions."

"That is easy to say when your ass isn't on the line," said Stella.

"But it will be," said Katie. "I'm coming along on this mission."

Hayden swallowed hard. He glanced at Stella, who stared at him, seeming to dare him to respond. Pavlovich rescued him.

"Okay, Thomas, let's assume for the moment this goofy plan will work and we'll get into Titan's atmosphere undetected. Then what?"

The admiral shrugged. "Fairly simple from that point; you land and deploy Rangers to enter and secure the facility. Once that is done, you retrieve the cynosure device and jump back here."

Pavlovich chuckled. "I suppose the damned thing is lying around and not under lock and key? It's a big place, from what I recall. It could be hidden anywhere. How large is it? How do we know it isn't broken up and scattered all over the place?"

"That is the other reason I am coming along," said Katie. "To answer your last question, Captain, the device *is* disassembled. I took it apart myself and stored it in a high-security locker, sealed with an encryption protocol of my own devising. Nothing short of a nuclear blast can rupture the casing. Though they tried to, they couldn't decrypt my pass code. It was removed to that facility and remains secured until they research a way to break into it. They won't succeed."

"That, ladies and gentlemen, is the plan," said Thomas. "The rest of our time here will be devoted to working out the tactical details among ourselves. Our intention is to set this in motion within forty-eight hours."

As people gathered into small specialty groups, Hayden studied Pavlovich. The big man did not appear pleased, but then he realized the captain was rarely happy with any plan but his own.

"What do you think?"

Pavlovich's frown lines deepened. "As plans go, it isn't a bad one."

"But?"

"But what? I can't think of any other way to recover the cynosure device, can you?"

Hayden shook his head. "Not really."

"Then this is a good plan by default. We'd best do our part to make sure it works, or everything we've done to get here is wasted effort."

With that, he rose and approached the cluster of people surrounding Thomas.

Hayden turned to Stella. "What do you think?"

She watched Katie, who was giving a lecture to a group of engineers. "I don't like the idea of her coming along."

"I told you, there is nothing between us."

She raised an eyebrow. "Of course there isn't. But there is something going on with her that her arrogant overconfidence can't hide, and it isn't fear of failure."

"Then what?"

"I don't know, but I'm going to keep my eye on her."

Setting the Board

HAYDEN FLEXED HIS SHOULDERS to test his mobility in the new jacket. As he checked himself out in the mirror, the buzzer sounded.

"Enter."

The door opened to reveal Kyle, sporting the same newly designed uniform.

He strode inside. "How's the fit? We only had your measurements from our academy days."

"It fits," said Hayden as he studied the unfamiliar crest where the UEF one should have been.

"Oh, and congratulations on your promotion, Commander Kaine."

His hand rose to touch the rank epaulet on his collar. "I'm not so sure that fits as well as the jacket."

"You earned it; you'll get used to the weight of it in time."

Hayden's eyes fell to Kyle's collar.

"Major Loram, is it?"

Kyle pointed to a badge on his chest. "I'm still with the Military Legal Office, though after a couple of jailbreaks and what we are about to do, I may have to apply for a transfer back to the less reputable space force, assuming I'm not arrested and tried for treason, that is."

"Well, this *is* all your idea," said Hayden with a wry smile. He slapped Kyle on the shoulder. "Anyway, you'll have to line up behind us other traitors. I must say, though, I'm surprised you are coming along on this mission, being a lawyer."

"Hey, I have a good head for tactics, and as you said, it's my plan. Besides, Thomas needs somebody representing him on *Scimitar*'s bridge."

Hayden relaxed his shoulders, relieved at the news. "The old goat should represent himself."

"He's almost eighty. He would like to come, but his granddaughter won't allow it."

"It doesn't sound like she's confident she's addressed the FTL problems. You might want to rethink your travel plans, just in case you intend to make little Kyles in the future."

"Katie says it won't be an issue. I think she's just being overprotective of the old man."

A brief silence fell. Hayden thought it strange that they had so little to talk about after being apart for so long.

"We should share a celebratory toast to our success," said Kyle. "I snuck a bottle of rum aboard."

"Wow, once you start breaking rules there is no stopping you. No thanks. I'm sworn off booze."

"Things really are changed."

Another silence descended.

"How long have you and Katie been together?"

"What?" said Kyle, shock on his face. "How did...?"

"Stella figured it out."

"I forgot she's an empath. That must make your relationship...interesting."

He smiled. "It presents challenges."

"I understand she has some particular abilities regarding the Malliac. It has something to do with her parents being exposed to something at an alien archaeological site, doesn't it?"

"How did you learn about that?"

"It was in Pavlovich's log."

Hayden nodded. *Of course it was.* "They activated some Glenatat technology at a xeno-archaeological dig while Stella's mother was pregnant with her."

He was uncomfortable discussing Stella. Thankfully, Pavlovich had shown some sense and kept the extent of her powers a secret. Only a couple of people were aware that her ability extended beyond what she could do to nearby Malliac. He wanted to keep things that way. Katie's interest in Cora was bad enough, but if Thomas learned what Stella could do to people with a cerebral LINK, he might find it tempting enough to violate her human rights. With that thought, Hayden confirmed how little he trusted Thomas. It was best that Kyle took his place on the mission.

"How extensive are her abilities?" said Kyle, interrupting Hayden's musing.

"The most she can do is sense them when they are near," he lied. "It gives us a heads up. The Glenatat tech is the real advantage we hold."

Kyle nodded. "Katie had a good look at that. We should be able to replicate it soon."

"Perhaps if we find success on this mission, the cynosure will eliminate the need."

Kyle frowned, making a face as if eating something distasteful. "I don't share Thomas's enthusiasm for the artifact's potential. It may be a transmitter to a long-dead race."

"The Glenatat disassembled it and hid the pieces."

"You met them, didn't you? What impression did you get from them to explain that?"

Hayden shook his head. "They are xenophobic in the extreme. I think they only agreed to help us because we were able to stop the Malliac from being a threat to them. If the cynosure could defend them, don't you think they'd have used it instead of relying on us? Maybe you're right and it will lead us to nothing helpful."

"But it must be of significance, Hayden. As you said, they went to a lot of trouble to hide it."

"I suppose we'll only solve this question after we've risked our lives to find the damned thing."

"If this is nothing but an elaborate practical joke, the weapons and tech aboard *Scimitar* are real enough. With time—"

"I don't believe there is enough time, Kyle. The best estimates put the Malliac on our doorstep in weeks. Even if Katie can replicate Glenatat technology, we are in no position to manufacture enough to make a difference against the entire horde. If this doesn't work out, we are all screwed."

Kyle pondered the thought for a moment. "Are you sure you don't want to reconsider joining me in a drink?"

"I'm tempted, friend. However, I've examined my problems from the bottom of more than a few empty bottles. Trust me when I tell you there are no answers to be found there."

They were interrupted by a voice over the speakers. "Excuse me, Commander Kaine... I like the sound of that."

Hayden smiled. "What can I do for you, Cora?"

"You and Major Loram are being called to the bridge. I believe the cap'n is ready to get underway."

"Thanks. Tell him we're on our way."

After she signed off, Kyle said, "Speaking of impressive technology, she is amazing. She sounds so cheerful, despite what she's been through."

Hayden winced. Everyone who encountered Cora since their arrival seemed to perceive her as nothing more than an exceptional technological feat.

"She's is a wonderful person."

"Yes, of course. I didn't mean—"

"She was different before this happened. You should visit her in her VR after this is over; both you and Katie should get to know her."

"Yeah, that sounds like a good idea. I look forward to the opportunity."

Hayden didn't worry about Kyle's perception of Cora. A few conversations with her and he'd see her for the person she was. Katie was a concern, however.

She'd changed.

She was still brilliant, but there was a hardness and arrogance to her that he did not recognize from a decade before. He had his doubts that she saw beyond the technology Cora had become, and that bothered him.

Perhaps he was allowing Stella's dislike for Katie to colour his own view of her, but he wasn't so sure.

Regardless, he decided she needed to be watched, if only to assure himself she posed no danger to Cora.

Squeezing Kyle on the shoulder, he said, "Shall we go? It's show-time."

• • • •

Wet sick covered the front of Kyle's new uniform.

Hayden couldn't help but smile to himself, despite his own queasi-ness.

A glance to the back of the bridge revealed that Katie hadn't vomit-ed, but she was pale and sweaty. Stella, sitting next to her, glanced back at Hayden and winked. She seemed smug.

He shook his head and frowned, wondering whether she had any-thing to do with Katie's discomfort. He wouldn't put it past her to have suggested Katie and Kyle sneak off for a quick breakfast together before departure, despite Hayden's warnings to them.

Pavlovich sat in the command chair, his nose wrinkled in disgust, though there was also a glint of amusement in his eye. Kyle was not the only one to embarrass himself. With *Scimitar*'s crew incarcerated on Earth, none of Thomas's people who now manned the ship had experi-enced the effects of an FTL jump before. To their credit, most managed to hold on to their stomach contents, but they all appeared worse for wear.

"Well done, people," said Pavlovich. His gaze fell on Kyle. "Well, most of you. Trust me when I say that this does not get any easier with experience. We've got some time before our next jump. Get yourselves cleaned up."

He motioned for Hayden to approach. "How did we do, Commander?"

"Cora says there is no structural damage, and nobody is reporting anything more severe than nausea. We can only hope the inoculations we all took worked."

Pavlovich looked at the crew. "From the looks of things, most people are okay. How are you feeling?"

"Better than previous jumps." He glanced at Kyle, who was mopping up his mess.

"This would be a lot better with our own people on the bridge. What is your assessment, Kaine? Are these people up to another jump?"

Hayden surveyed the crew. "We have some recovery time. Ships from Titan won't arrive here for another couple of hours. My concern is the fighting fitness of our new team of Rangers after our transit."

"I'm not worried about them. They're a tough lot and will suck it up to get the job done. Most of them have probably gone into combat hungover more than a few times. My bigger worry is about jumping into Titan's atmosphere."

"We arrived here within metres of our intended coordinates, essentially a bull's-eye. I don't foresee any problems."

"Then I guess I'll authorize the mission to proceed. Deploy our drones to begin pretending to be Malliac."

"Aye-aye, Captain."

Pavlovich settled back into his chair. "Now we wait."

Lifting the Veil

TWO HOURS AND TWENTY minutes later, Hayden's eyes were riveted on the holographic imager, trying to pierce through opaque, swirling clouds of orange and blue.

"We are at the predetermined coordinates in Titan's atmosphere, Captain," said the helmsman. Hayden noted that he and the rest of the bridge crew had fared the second jump better than the first.

A quick glance to Kyle and Katie showed them conversing, unaffected.

"Any sensor contacts, Mister Kaine?" asked Pavlovich.

Redirecting his attention to the instruments, he confirmed his initial readings. "No sign that we've been spotted, Captain, but sensors are compromised by the atmosphere."

"If we can't see them, then they certainly won't spy us. Helm, begin descent to the ground coordinates." He hit a button on his chair and announced over the ship's address system, "All hands, rig for landing. Rangers report to your muster stations."

He appraised Hayden. "Time to go, Commander Kaine. Good hunting."

"Tsk, Captain," said Katie as she joined them. "Do I detect envy? Did you want to heroically lead the charge?"

"I'm getting too old for such shenanigans. My XO is the perfect choice for the job."

"Of course he is," she said. "I assigned everyone according to their skills."

"In your estimation, I'm sure that is the case. I'm just not comfortable with the idea of you tagging along. You have no combat experience."

She frowned. "I have first-hand knowledge about the cynosure device. My presence is required."

"I can't guarantee your safety, and if your grandfather finds out I endangered you..."

"You should worry about what he will do if he learns you interfered with the recovery plan."

Pavlovich flushed, and his frown turned to a scowl. Without taking his eyes off of her, he said, "Mister Kaine, you had best take this young woman to the armoury and fit her for light armour. She has a job to do, and we wouldn't want anything so mundane as a stray bullet to prevent her from doing it."

Hayden gently touched Katie's elbow to prompt her. She pulled her gaze from the captain and acknowledged the first officer with a curt nod before heading for the hatchway.

"Try to keep someone from shooting her, Kaine, for all of our sakes."

He tried to suppress his smile. "I'll do my best, sir." He then walked to where Stella stood with Kyle.

She wrapped her arms around Hayden's neck and pulled him in for a lingering hug. After they reluctantly ended their embrace, he turned to Kyle. He was at a loss for words. Katie had departed without so much as a glance at him.

"Take care of her, Hayden," he said. "There is a lot riding on her shoulders." He said it as if it explained her actions.

"I'll get her back safe and sound."

"Make sure you bring yourself back," Stella told him, a frown creasing her brow.

He smiled, and, after kissing her, left the bridge and hurried to join Katie.

Catching up with her just outside of the armoury, he said, "What is going on between you two?"

"He's a pretentious oaf."

"Kyle?"

Her face reddened, and she quickly turned away to hide her embarrassment. "No, Pavlovich."

"I don't think you know him well enough to make that call. Is that your opinion or your grandfather's?"

She said nothing as she opened the door and entered.

Shaking his head, he followed her inside and proceeded to the equipment locker.

Silently, he began removing kit and handing it to her to try on.

"Kyle and I said our goodbyes earlier this morning," she said, "as if it is any of your business."

"It isn't."

He moved to a different locker.

"Do you enjoy needling him?" he asked without turning to look at her.

"Kyle?"

He frowned. "Pavlovich."

"You wouldn't understand."

He slammed down the helmet he held and turned to face her. "Why don't you humour me and try explaining it? Use small words if you think it might help."

"Hayden, I really don't think this the appropriate time or place to discuss it."

He crossed his arms. "It certainly is. I'm about to take you into a combat situation, and at the very least, I must be confident that you and Thomas don't have a plan to screw Pavlovich or me. I can't afford any doubt, so I will make it easy for you. Tell me what the hell is going on, or I'll order you to be left behind."

"You can't do that. I'm in charge of this mission."

"Only until we step outside of the ship. Then I'm the task force commander, and your presence falls under my discretion. What's it to be?"

She sighed. "Hayden, I realize he is your captain, but your loyalty is misplaced."

"In whose estimation? Your grandfather's? He's the one who tried to recruit Pavlovich into a conspiracy to take over the government."

Katie raised an eyebrow. "Is that what you were told? That isn't what happened."

"You weren't there."

Her expression softened. "Hayden, you weren't either."

He frowned. "This is pointless. Neither of us trusts the other's source for this story."

He turned back to the locker and began putting on his armour. He couldn't bring himself to look at her, but he heard her begin dressing behind him. She hadn't told him anything new except that the admiral's version of what went down between him and Pavlovich differed in some way. The notion that Pavlovich's side of the story was embellished to place him in the more favourable light had occurred to him more than once.

He decided that the mystery of the true nature of the relationship between the two men could wait. He had to keep his focus on the mission at hand or more would suffer than his trust in the captain.

Heavy, clanking footfalls echoed in the corridor before the hatch opened. A combat synth loomed in the doorway; its lifeless eyes focused on Hayden.

Cora's voice came through the android's mouth. "The Rangers are waiting."

He fastened the last clasp on his jacket and stood. "I'm ready."

Katie rose and donned her helmet. "We both are."

Hayden returned her defiant gaze.

"Is there a problem?" she asked.

"No. Cora, would you please escort the doctor to the staging area? I'm putting her under your direct care."

"No problem, Commander."

After they departed, Hayden took a moment to remove and check his sidearm. As he stared at the gun, he realized that for the first time since meeting her, he no longer trusted Katie, or even liked her.

Stella, of course, had never been shy of expressing that opinion, but he credited that to jealousy. He'd defended Katie's arrogance in response to Stella's uncharacteristic dislike for her, but he now appreciated that something was wrong. Stella's empathic senses detected in his old girlfriend what he refused to see until now.

It wasn't that Katie had changed in ten years. Far from it—her attitude toward those she saw as her inferiors was as he always remembered. He never acknowledged the behaviour as the serious character flaw that it was.

He wondered if Kyle accepted it, or like him, was wilfully blinded to her inner ugliness by her striking beauty. He shook his head in sorrow for his old friend.

He was grateful for his epiphany. Now he could view her as a member of the team, no more special than anyone else. He was free to focus on his mission without fearing she would be a distraction.

Slipping the pistol back into its holster, he exited into the corridor. If everything went as planned, the cynosure device would soon be in his possession.

That was the easier part than what was to follow.

He had no idea who he could trust enough to hand over such a key to power.

SCIMITAR set down half a kilometre away from the facility. It was the closest Pavlovich dared take the ship lest even their Glenatat modifications fail to conceal them from the station's sensors.

The frozen ground crunched under boots as the squad of ten trudged through the toxic fog that obscured their path. Guided by the topographic model projected onto their HUDS, they cautiously made their way to the station.

Upon arriving, Cora scanned the facility with her built in instruments to confirm the facility's security sensor coverage matched the details Thomas had supplied. She activated the decoy signal to mask their approach and, with weapons at the ready, the team advanced to the access point.

The anxious moments waiting to learn if the pilfered codes supplied by Thomas were valid quickly evaporated when the surface access door opened to admit them.

Wordlessly, Cora's avatar advanced to the control panel so she could establish contact with defence grid and disable it. Normally, such a thing would be impossible. Cora's unique nature, however, was nothing the system's designers had anticipated.

After three long minutes, she rose to her feet and gave Hayden the thumbs-up.

"I'm in. I'm partitioned and running through their internal network. All the security traps are disabled, and I'll remain inside their system to make sure we aren't detected."

"The base's AI was no problem?"

"Naw, we're becoming best buddies. You'll only have to worry about the roaming human teams. I can track them, but you'll have to deal with them."

He frowned. "You're not coming?"

The combat synth shrugged. "I have to remain here to keep pinging the physical connection, otherwise I'll be trapped in the network. There is no other way."

"I'll leave someone here to watch your back."

"Don't be silly." Cora's android form towered over him. "I can defend myself just fine. Besides, you can't afford to be down two this early in the mission. I'll be okay."

He glanced at the eight other members then gave the order for the airlock's inner door to be opened.

Weapons at the ready, the advance team filed out until only Hayden and Katie remained. He motioned for her to proceed.

It was difficult for him to see her expression behind her tinted helmet visor, but Hayden thought she appeared uncertain. Before he could encourage her, though, she stepped through the door and into the corridor beyond. He followed with the soldiers on his heels.

The column silently advanced through the dimly illuminated labyrinth of corridors, following the coded homing beacon Katie had programmed into the package they now sought.

It wasn't long before Cora spoke into his helmet receiver. "Heads up. An armed security team is around the next corner, heading your way."

Wordlessly, everyone pressed against the walls. The two lead Rangers knelt in a firing position, flechette rifles trained on the intersection ahead.

Hayden tightened his grip on his weapon, wishing he were close enough to shield Katie from potential fire and debating the wisdom of moving forward to do so.

Before he could do anything, two figures rounded the corner and were felled by needle projectiles that tore through their armour as if through paper.

With chilling efficiency, two Rangers hurried to secure the adjoining corridor while another pair silently removed the bodies to a less conspicuous location in a doorway.

Hayden was surprised by how little blood marked where the guards fell. The high-temperature needles cauterized the wounds as they made them, making their deaths almost bloodless.

"All clear on this level," said Cora.

Hayden signalled for the squad to continue to their objective. He passed Katie to ensure she would not risk being exposed to a potential exchange of fire again. He assuaged his growing internal conflict by telling himself that he did so for the good of the mission; if she fell, there would be no way to open the sealed case that held the device.

True to Cora's prediction, the team met nobody else before they arrived at the lift that would take them into the core of the facility. As if by magic, the elevator doors parted under Cora's command. Two Rangers entered it ahead of Katie and Hayden, the four almost filling the car to capacity. The doors closed, and they began to descend.

This was the part of the operation that gave Hayden the most cause for concern. The plans for the upper few levels of the station were, while not common knowledge, at least familiar to most senior commanders. What lay beneath was classified at a level above even that of Admiral Thomas. Only the command officers of the Titan armoury were privy to the inner configuration of the base. Even then, humans rarely set foot there. Access was kept exclusive to synths under the control of the base's AI.

Fortunately, that complication was being handled.

Hayden spoke into his helmet pickup. "How are we looking, Cora?"

"Umm, okay. The base AI is being a little bit difficult."

His throat constricted. "What's going on?"

"She's just more sophisticated than I was led to believe. I need to be on my toes more than I expected. Nothing that I can't handle."

"You're sure?"

"Nothing to worry about, Commander. I'll inform you if the situation changes."

Not feeling assured, he ended their side conversation as the elevator slowed.

The doors parted to blackness.

Switching to IR display, he couldn't make out anything. He debated the wisdom of activating his helmet light when gridlines resolved in front of him as Cora began to interpret the environment for him and the others and display it on their HUDs. Before his eyes, a brightly lit corridor appeared, walls marked at equal intervals by fortified doors.

Katie pushed past him and the soldiers. Hayden and one of the Rangers followed her while the other remained to keep the lift secured.

Fearlessly, she strode down the hallway and around a corner until she finally halted before a door.

"Are you sure this is the one?"

Before she could answer, the locking mechanism on the door clicked and the bolts slid back under Cora's command. Katie reached to pull open the massive door without waiting for help.

Beyond the entrance lay a vast, empty circular chamber, over twenty metres in diameter. Inset into the walls were dozens of wide doors, all of them with an inset keypad containing a hundred buttons. Instead of alphanumeric characters, unfamiliar hieroglyphs were imprinted on each key.

"Which one, Cora?" There was unmistakable excitement in Katie's voice.

"J..st give me a second."

A moment later, a keypad began to blink. Katie hurried toward the door.

"Do you have the access code?" she asked.

"Yppp."

Random lights flashed on the keypad as Cora activated a complex sequence.

Nothing happened.

"Cora?" said Hayden.

"Sorry, I... wait...Okay, there it izzz."

"Is something wrong?"

As if in reply, the keys flashed in a second attempt.

The mechanism clicked, and the door sprang away from the wall.

Katie pulled it open and entered.

Hayden checked that the Ranger still maintained a watch on the entrance to the corridor before following her into the chamber.

Inside, she knelt before a long, cylindrical object that was large enough for Cora's combat synth to comfortably lie down in. She removed her helmet and gloves, then pressed her palm against the interface embedded on its side. Following that, she lowered her face to it to be retina scanned. When the panel flashed green, she straightened her back and her fingers flew over the keypad.

"Is that your security locker?"

"Shh, I'm trying to concentrate."

He reined in his anxiety and waited as she worked intently. Finally, when he thought she forgot her decryption key, the top of the unit slid open. She reached inside and pulled out a backpack.

"You're kidding. The cynosure device is in that?"

Annoyance crossed her face, and she started to reply, but was interrupted when the lighting in the chamber flickered. Hayden looked nervously around the room as the walls wavered, like disturbed pond surface.

"Cora, what's going on?" he said.

She didn't answer, and without taking the time to repeat himself, he grabbed Katie by the upper arm and pulled her to her feet.

"Something's wrong. We need to get the hell out of here." He picked up her helmet from the floor and shoved it into her hands.

"Now!" he shouted as he pushed her toward the door.

Before they could take two steps, they were plunged into blackness.

"HAYDEN! WHERE ARE YOU?"

Katie's voice sounded muffled, as if she were in another room.

Unable to see, he activated his IR display, but it made no difference; the material of the walls, ceiling, and floor rendered the technology useless. Turning on his helmet light, he was shocked to discover it didn't work.

He initially guessed that something had deactivated it when an oddity caught his attention. Shining the light on his hand, he could only make out a grey smudge. Pulling the helmet off, he shone the beam in his face. A deep grey circle hung in the blackness where a blinding beam should have been. He moved it closer until it almost touched his nose, but the area only lightened slightly. Whatever security technology was employed, he'd seen nothing like it before. It was as if the surroundings were absorbing every photon, leaving nothing visible.

"Follow my voice," he shouted.

Moments later, something brushed against his sleeve before desperate hands latched onto his arm.

"What happened?" Gone was her arrogance as her fingers dug into him. Even next to him, Katie's voice sounded as if it came from a great distance. Hayden realized the room must be absorbing sound waves as well.

"I'm not sure. There is dampening technology down here that I'm not familiar with. It's probably rendered our communications useless as well. Something happened to Cora. The VR display she was generating for us went out."

He called out, "Sergeant Schotzky, can you hear me?"

"Yes, sir." The Ranger's voice was muffled.

"Are you still in position by the door?"

"Yes, sir."

"Good, keep speaking. We're going to make our way to you."

He and Katie followed Schotzky's voice in the darkness. Hayden was amazed by the ice water that seemed to flow through the sergeant's veins. He began to believe that if the other members of his team were like him, there might still be a chance for them to escape.

With Katie attached to his arm like a lamprey, he shuffled forward, maintaining a conversation with Schotzky, letting his voice guide them. After an unbearably long and slow journey, his outstretched arm contacted the soldier.

"What is the plan, sir?"

"Was it Beech who came down here with us?"

"Yes, Commander."

"Beech! Can you hear me?"

A long pause ensued, and he repeated his call.

A very faint voice called back.

Hayden told Schotzky, "I want you two to shout at each other. Get him to lead us to him. I'm going to try and raise Cora."

Katie's shaking hands squeezed his arm in a death grip. He turned to her and tried to speak softly into her ear. When that failed, he reluctantly resorted to a bar room shout. "Take slow, deep breaths and focus on putting one foot in front of the other. Grab Schotzky with your other hand and let him lead us back the way we came."

As the three of them shuffled along in the darkness, Hayden lowered his visor and flipped through the comm channels, trying to find one that would let him speak to Cora.

After several fruitless minutes, their surroundings brightened slightly. A faint yellow grid appeared on his HUD where the walls and floor should have been.

"Cora?"

"Hayden, is everyone okay?"

"We're fine. What's happened?"

"It's this AI. I underestimated her. She's trying to wrest control of the system and is erecting firewalls to isolate me. I'm managing to knock them down, but she's far more powerful than I realized. I can't guess how much time I have before she overwhelms me. You need to get out of there."

"We have what we came for and are nearly at the lift."

"Hurry. She's activated security protocols. I'm trying to counteract them and hide your presence but zheez got too many backup rez-zorzesssss..."

"Cora?"

"Zzzzzt* I'm sorry Hayden. I have to cut off comms if I want to keep the lights on for you. Hurry. I'll hold her off as long as I can."

The channel went dead, not even the static hiss of a lost signal coming through.

Hayden told the others to lower their visors so they could see the VR surroundings. They ran in the direction of the elevator. Beech waited for them, still calling into the darkness. Hayden kept checking behind them, weapon at the ready to cover their retreat, but nothing followed.

They pushed inside, and the doors closed. As they began their upward journey, Hayden prayed that Cora could stay in control long enough to get them to the surface level, where they would at least be able to see what the base's AI might send at them.

He tried unsuccessfully to raise *Scimitar* before realizing that the same dampening technology in the lower levels prevented communications with the ship. They could not call for support and would be on their own if the need arose to fight their way out against an AI sophisticated enough to overwhelm Cora. He didn't like their chances.

It had been shocking for him to hear the fear in her voice. Even though she was partitioned and could theoretically survive the loss of that fragment of herself if things went wrong, he was worried for her. His original confidence that her Glenatat technology could prevail against anything mere humans might invent was shattered. He now feared for her existence.

A quick glance at the overhead light in the elevator car gave him a bit of hope. The enemy AI had not yet located them. That meant Cora might still be unharmed, but he knew it wouldn't be for much longer.

The lift jerked to a halt. Everyone raised a weapon in anticipation of an awaiting security detachment.

An empty corridor greeted them. A red light pulsed in time with a klaxon. Somewhere in the distance, there was gunfire from the direction of their escape. Hayden automatically checked his HUD for life signs from his team, but like communication with *Scimitar*, those signals were blocked.

The Rangers' orders for the mission were simple enough. They were responsible for maintaining an exit corridor for the retrieval team. The fact that a battle was taking place somewhere deep in the facility told Hayden they were still alive. Unfortunately, it also came from where they needed to go.

As per protocol, Schotzky assumed point while Beech guarded their backs.

The corridors they passed through were empty, though as they advanced Hayden noted increasing signs of recent combat. Scorch markings and small arms damage peppered the hallway. When they were close to the airlock, Schotzky raised his fist and they stopped. Cautiously, he opened his visor and turned his head to listen.

Hayden mimicked him and strained his ears for what had garnered the Ranger's attention.

"What's happened?" whispered Katie.

"Shh," hissed Schotzky. After a few more seconds, he looked at them. "The fighting stopped."

Hayden checked his HUD, but there was still no signal and no way to determine who remained alive only a few dozen metres around the next corner.

"Well, we can't stay here." Katie's condescending tone had returned.

Hayden bit his lip and suppressed the urge to suggest she take the lead.

More diplomatically, the sergeant said, "We have to establish if the route is clear, ma'am." He turned to Hayden. "With your permission, sir?"

He nodded, and the Ranger lowered his visor before he motioned for the group to advance toward the intersection.

Hayden's heart pounded out of control, and a bead of sweat ran down his cheek. He anticipated base security to be waiting for them the moment they poked their heads around the corner.

Halting just before they would be exposed, Schotzky removed a marble-sized sphere from his utility belt. A video feed popped up on Hayden's helmet display just as the sergeant rolled the device around the corner.

Instead, of overwhelming numbers of soldiers, what showed up on the screen was mayhem.

The lower torso of one of his Rangers lay sprawled in a bloody pool, everything missing above his waist. There was nobody else in the area.

Hayden jumped when Katie's fingers gripped his arm. Too late he realized that her HUD was also active, and she was witnessing the same horrifying scene. To her credit, she did not panic.

Following Schotzky's lead, he raised his weapon and followed him around the corner. He couldn't pull his eyes from the mutilated corpse. Ten metres farther up the corridor, the rest of the hapless Ranger lay propped against the wall, as if tossed there.

The only thing that could do that kind of damage was a combat mech, but the corridors were too low and narrow to accommodate one. Whatever killed the man, and probably the rest of his team, was something he'd never encountered.

As they advanced down the passage, they came across more bodies. The first thing Hayden realized was that there were too many. With Cora left behind at the interface near the airlock, only five of his team had remained up top. There were twice that number of corpses littering the floor only metres ahead of them.

One or two displayed similar signs of violence, legs and arms torn off and cast aside. One or two of the Ranger bodies showed nonlethal projectile wounds from weapons fire.

The remains of the base's security forces were far more badly mutilated than all but the first Ranger they'd found.

Katie, still clinging to Hayden's arm, whispered to him, "Something interrupted the firefight."

"It was big and nasty," he replied.

After having thoroughly checked the area beyond the carnage, Schotzky returned to speak to them while a nervous-looking Beech stood watch.

"Everyone is dead."

"What did this?"

The sergeant shook his head. "I dunno, sir, but the twenty metres to the airlock is clear. We should go."

Gunfire erupted behind them.

They all turned in time to see Beech lifted from the floor and hurled into the wall like a broken doll.

A large, menacing humanoid silhouette towered above them for a moment before lunging at Katie.

Schotzky pushed her aside and unloaded his weapon at the advancing horror. Armour-piercing rounds tore into the damaged torso of the beast as its hand reached up and seized the top of the sergeant's head.

A sickening crunch filled the air as helmet and skull caved beneath the pressure of the monster's grip. It grasped Schotzky's still kicking leg with its other arm and ripped the remains of his head away.

After tossing the decapitated corpse aside, it turned once again to Katie.

Hayden fired round after round at the creature's head until it turned its attention to him.

A single lifeless eye within a mutilated face fixed on him.

The machine stopped, as if uncertain of how to proceed.

Buzzing noises, like a malfunctioning communications unit, came from the android's destroyed mouth. Hayden heard a faint, static garbled message in his helmet receiver. The voice in his ear sounded familiar, and as the combat synth continued to remain unmoving, he risked a glance at the HUD to identify the source of the signal.

He gasped and stepped back a pace, weapon still pointed at the machine. He raised his visor and searched for his voice.

"Cora?"

Heavy Price

THE HULKING RUIN OF the combat synth teetered before its knees buckled and it collapsed to the floor. Its limbs spasmed, and it uttered incomprehensible noises.

"Hayden, is that Cora?" Katie's eyes were wide in shock.

"Yes." He lowered his weapon and moved a step closer. "She's trying to communicate, but the dampening field is still jamming our comms."

Katie studied the damaged visage of Cora's avatar as the pitiful remnant of its mouth moved noiselessly. After seeming to decide, she knelt next to it and examined the machine's torso. "Help me turn her over."

Puzzled, Hayden holstered his gun and joined her at Cora's side. "What are you looking for?"

"These units have an auxiliary access portal. She wants to talk to us."

Together, they struggled to roll the machine onto its side, and Katie continued her examination.

"Here it is. It doesn't seem damaged."

She retrieved a small tool kit from her utility pouch. After opening the access port and making adjustments, she pulled a wire from the kit and attached it to a terminal.

"What's that?" asked Hayden.

"The dampening field won't allow wireless comms, so I am going to make a hardwire connection." She began to attach the other end to her helmet. Hayden reached over and stopped her.

"It should be me."

"Together, Cora and I can address what caused her to malfunction."

Hayden shook his head, a tear running down his cheek. "She doesn't want that." He gently took the wire from her hand and connected it to his helmet. He thought of closing his visor to keep their conversation private, then reconsidered and invited Katie to lean close to listen in.

"Cora, are you there?"

"Hayden, I...I..."

She couldn't cry, at least not like she once might have. The synth had no ability to mimic it, and he wasn't sure if her virtual world sufficiently replicated the biochemistry that resulted in the same emotional outlet shedding tears might provide.

"It's okay, Cora. Tell me what happened."

"I don't have much time. The base's AI was too powerful for me. I was overpowered and forced to exit the system. I heard the gunshots and ran to help our people. Together, we managed to hold back the security forces and seal off this section of the base from reinforcements."

Hayden glanced over at the bodies strewn around the floor and imagined the battle while she spoke.

"But I made a mistake. It followed me, infiltrated my synth, and took over. Hayden, it was so horrible. I tried to find different back routes, erected firewalls, but none of it did any good. I couldn't do anything to stop it. I had to watch while it did those things to our people."

"But you finally stopped it, Cora. You're back."

The machine struggled to shake its head, and its body twitched. Startled, both he and Katie moved back.

"No, I only managed to confuse it, thanks to you. The sight of you accessed some pathways the AI hadn't discovered. I won't have control for long. I can already feel it breaking through."

"We can save you, Cora. Tell us what to do."

"Go! Get out of here and back to *Scimitar* as fast as you can; before they breach our security seals on the door. I don't know what this system has in reserve, but you won't survive it."

"But we can't abandon you here."

"You must. There is no other way. Take the cynosure device and complete the mission."

"But what happens if we leave you? What will losing this partition do to you?"

"Hayden, I really don't know, but this synth is beyond repair, and you can't carry it."

Katie rummaged through her utility pouch. "Perhaps we can extract her core consciousness. I have a portable storage unit here."

"No, that won't work. The AI has infected and begun to fragment me. If you take me back, I will contaminate all of *Scimitar*'s systems if I recombine. Leave me."

"But Cora ...," said Hayden.

"It's okay. I'm confident that my partition on the ship will function fine without me. It won't remember any of this. There is no way you can risk uploading anything from this mission. Optical logs, sensor records...all of it must be destroyed. This AI is powerful, and you can't give it any avenue to infiltrate *Scimitar*."

An explosion echoed from the other side of a wall farther down the corridor.

"There is not much time," said Cora. "Find the cynosure. Save humanity."

Another, louder boom shook the floor.

Katie's hand squeezed Hayden's arm. "We should go."

He nodded, tears fogging his vision. "Goodbye."

"You'll see me again in a few minutes. It will be like this never happened. I'm going to shut down now to give you a bit more time before the AI reboots me. Go, save the universe."

What he once considered a lifeless eye on the synth seemed to die, and Cora's body stopped twitching.

Katie pulled him to his feet, and they ran to the exit point. He felt numb inside at the loss of his team, but mostly over losing Cora. The sad part was that she was right. The remnant of her consciousness was still intact and functioning on the ship. The dead Rangers, however, did not have that second chance.

As the airlock depressurized, he was grateful his visor hid his tears. He wondered how many more lives would be lost before this was over.

The Cynosure

HAYDEN AND PAVLOVICH entered the large chamber hollowed out of the middle of Thomas's asteroid. It was twenty metres in diameter, and its walls were sheathed in surplus gravity plating that had been scavenged from every ship in their small fleet. The entire structure was constructed around the alien machine that was now suspended in the centre of the space, secured by a complex artificial gravitational field.

Pavlovich whistled softly. "To think this was solid rock a week ago. This is bloody impressive."

Hayden surveyed the engineering achievement emotionlessly. "I hope this is worth all we've been through."

The captain's hand rested on Hayden's shoulder. "The Malliac have not left us much of a choice. I consider it providential that we've achieved this much. Aren't you a little bit excited about what will happen when we turn it on?"

"I think there is still the chance we've built a doomsday device that will snuff us out along with the Malliac."

Pavlovich's expression softened. This conversation was a familiar one.

It had been eight standard days since *Scimitar* jumped from the surface of Titan and returned to the belt. On their arrival, the admiral was giddy with triumph, barely taking the time to acknowledge the men and women who paid the ultimate price for his prize.

Even Katie, up to her nose in the carnage, compartmentalized her emotions much too quickly as far as Hayden was concerned. She joined Thomas in making plans to assemble the device, both vanishing into the laboratory almost as soon as the ship docked. She expressed no concern for Cora's loss and didn't offer any comment on the Rangers who gave their lives for her protection. Even Kyle could come up with no words to excuse the callous obsession she shared with her grandfather.

Though they were not part of his original crew, Pavlovich joined Hayden in grieving for the fallen. Together, they planned the memorial service while Stella spoke with those who needed to talk about the loss. He couldn't shake the feeling the price paid was too low and that a yet-to-be-assessed debt was coming due.

Footfalls behind them announced the arrival of the others who were selected to witness the pending historical moment.

The admiral strode in, back straight and proud. At his side was his granddaughter. Katie's pride was less obvious, but Hayden knew her well enough to tell she was basking in what she considered her achievement. Memories of Schotzky and Beech momentarily hijacked Hayden's attention before he pushed them to the back of his mind to deal with later.

On the heels of the triumphant pair followed Kyle, like a royal consort. Hayden frowned at his uncharitable assessment of their relationship, but he couldn't bring himself to think it wasn't true.

As they assumed their places around the device, Stella and Eli entered, engaged in a deep discussion. She looked at Hayden, as if his thoughts and feelings had struck her across the face. Her expression of surprise softened, and she smiled as she approached.

"Sorry," he whispered to her as the scent of her shampoo wafted to his nose. Its familiarity quieted his troubled mind, and Stella's shoulders relaxed as his own emotions settled.

Her reply was to discreetly clasp his hand and stand closer to him.

Pavlovich leaned forward and spoke softly. "If you two need to get a room..."

Stella rolled her eyes while Hayden shook his head and suppressed a smile.

Eli joined them when he finished conversing with Kyle. "I've not seen you to congratulate you on your success, nephew."

"To be honest, uncle, I wasn't all that useful." He nodded in Katie's direction. "That young woman deserves most of the credit."

Eli snorted and patted Hayden on the shoulder. "Time will tell whether there is recognition or blame to be portioned out. Be grateful for your present place in shadows."

"I'm not..."

Smiling, Eli waved his hand dismissively and smiled, as if his comment was but a joke. He moved down the line to talk to someone else.

Disturbed, Hayden turned to Stella. "I'm not envious."

She raised her eyebrow and squeezed his hand patronizingly.

He was about to argue his case when Admiral Thomas cleared his throat in preparation to address the assembly.

"Thank you, everyone, for attending this historic occasion. Many have sacrificed so that humanity now has this opportunity. Today, their spilled blood will open a gate to the gods and to the means for us to defend ourselves and rebuild our empire."

Hayden winced at the poorly chosen analogy. Thomas should save the bad rhetoric for the political arena. Most people assembled here were technical or military specialists, and he doubted many wished to listen to bullshit. A quick glance about confirmed his suspicion. Many looked uncomfortable with the admiral's words.

Seeming to recognize his lack of rapport with his audience, the admiral stuffed the page with his prepared remarks into his jacket and invited Katie to explain and demonstrate the device.

She stepped forward with an aura of confidence that was familiar to Hayden. He recalled many an evening while they were seeing each other when she regaled him with impromptu lectures about her latest work. At the time, her little performances enthralled and amused him. She'd dazzled him with her brilliance, and he felt privileged to be associated with such an Olympian as her.

But now, to him, her glow was not so bright, and her confidence came across as arrogant self-importance. He looked around the crowd and wondered how many others saw what he did. Who of them was enraptured with her as he had once been?

A tug on his hand told him at least one other person shared his assessment. He gently squeezed Stella's fingers, and a conspiratorial smile turned up the corner of her mouth, as if they were privy to a scandalous secret.

He suddenly realized he hadn't been listening to Katie. Considering what was at stake, he believed he should try to pay attention to her. She might be arrogant, but that did not diminish her intellect.

"The machine suspended before you is a projection device. I won't bore you with the operational details behind it, because we do not yet understand some of it..."

That was an understatement. Cora had told Hayden that even with her intimate relationship with Glenatat technology, she had difficulty with the math. She explained that the human mind was not capable of conceiving what was necessary to describe the physics. Humans were restricted by biology and incapable of perceiving how much of the universe works.

The reason the cynosure device would function at all was not due to Katie's understanding of the science, but rather because the Glenatat had designed it to. Human monkeys only had to put the puzzle together and turn the thing on.

The difficult part was anticipating what that action would do. If time had permitted, years of testing would have revealed what was now in front of them. Humanity had not been afforded that luxury, so a more desperate risk had to be taken.

Hayden realized his past actions were the primary reason for the present desperation. In solving one problem, he'd created other, larger ones.

"Commander Kaine?"

It took him a moment to realize he was being called. He looked up to everyone staring at him.

"Hayden," said Katie, "will you please come forward to activate the cynosure device?"

"Uh, certainly." He straightened his jacket. With a last glance at Stella, he moved through the crowd to join Katie and the admiral beneath the machine.

He stared up at the apparatus with its alien markings, captivated by its strange beauty. Katie nudged him and handed him a small control. He turned it over, hands shaking as he examined it.

"Ah, you're sure this thing won't explode when I turn it on?"

Though his question was serious, a few chuckled. Though Katie shared in the laughter, her eyes told him she was not pleased.

"That is very funny, Commander, but I want to assure everyone once again that this device is only an activation node. We tuned it to direct a signal to coordinates two hundred thousand kilometres from here. One of our ships is stationed at that point and is relaying data back to us here." She pointed to the holographic projector next to them, which displayed a vista of stars as seen from the observation ship.

He silently wondered which hapless ship's crew had been selected for the assignment.

Chuckling, he said, "Well, like many, I was never the most attentive of students." The crowd was in a generous mood and laughed at his joke.

The embarrassing moment over, he examined the device in his hand and swallowed while trying to work up the nerve to do what was asked of him. When he thought Katie would lose her cool and grab it from him, he raised the control and theatrically pressed the activation button for all to see.

All eyes turned to the hologram projector.

The image of the star field remained annoyingly static, but he felt he dared not blink lest any sign of his doubt might somehow jinx the demonstration.

Time passed. The people became restless as the display stubbornly refused to change.

Katie spoke into a headset he hadn't seen her don. "What are the other spectral bands showing? Are you sure? We don't see any of that here..."

Somebody shouted, "There!"

Hayden stared at the image, desperate for any indication that they had not fallen for an elaborate alien practical joke.

The stars in the middle of the display softened and flowed around an unseen central point. As they circled, their light smeared behind them like running paint. With increasing speed, the star field turned until individual trails blurred into each other and the region became an amorphous hole of spinning white light.

The white began to disperse like a fog, revealing a yellow sun, disappointingly familiar-looking.

The room buzzed. Questions and speculative answers filled the air as everyone tried to puzzle through what they saw. Some voiced concern that they were somehow looking at an image of the Sol system through an alien imaging device.

Katie held one hand to the headset, the other raised to try to attract everyone's attention. "The spectral analysis confirms this is not our sun." Excitement and relief were in her voice.

Hayden allowed himself to hope. If it was an alien system, then the stories and myths were true, and they'd opened a doorway to another star system. Perhaps they might yet find something to help them fight the Malliac. At the very least, it might provide a way for people to escape the invading horde.

But there were too many questions. Where was the star? If there was an advanced civilization on the other side of that hole, were they friendly or more dangerous than those who now threatened them? Hayden's mind was awhirl with conflicting emotions.

He looked over at Stella. She clutched at her temples, trying to cope with everyone experiencing the same confusion as him.

Katie's voice cut through his mental clutter. "They are launching a probe into the portal."

Portal, Hayden thought, *they already have an explanation, even though they are clueless what they are dealing with. I wonder who they plan to name it after?*

The probe approached the hole in space, and he prepared for the possibility that it might explode or bounce off what was nothing more than a window nobody could pass through.

It did neither, crossing the event threshold without incident, and continued through toward the alien sun.

"We continue to receive telemetry," said Katie. "It appears we discovered a gateway to another star system."

A cheer rang up from the crowd.

Hayden joined with them, hoping against hope that they had not opened a door onto a greater threat.

Desperation

"COMMANDER KAINE, YOU'VE not touched your Scotch."

Hayden leaned forward to put the glass on the admiral's desk. "I'm waiting for something to celebrate."

His commitment to sobriety aside, he thought he could really use a drink and just wanted the temptation out of reach. His suspicion of the admiral didn't help. He and Pavlovich had been called to his office following the demonstration, without any explanation. He didn't believe Thomas liked either of them enough to warrant sharing a private libation, so something else was up.

"Kaine's right, Robert, that was a gutsy gamble." Pavlovich's feet were perched on the edge of the desk and his second glass of whisky almost drained. "It could have flopped or blown up in your face. What the hell were you thinking?"

"The time for caution is over." Thomas sat across from them, slouched in his chair, his collar open. Though he gave the impression of someone ready to celebrate, his manner was anything but festive. "We are out of time." He tossed a dossier across the desk. "We've sighted the Malliac fleet."

Eyes wide, Pavlovich sat straight and grabbed the document. "Where?"

"They are converging on two fronts; the details are in that. The point is that they are coming, and we now have a definite timeline for their arrival."

"How long?" said Hayden.

"Their first vessels will enter Pluto's orbit in six weeks."

"How many?" asked Pavlovich.

Thomas sighed and leaned forward to pour himself another drink. He pushed the bottle back to Pavlovich. "The latest estimate puts their number at ninety thousand, but that keeps going up every day."

"Shit." Pavlovich's shoulders slumped. "How long have you known?"

Thomas shrugged. "Two days, not that telling anyone sooner would make a difference." He chuckled mirthlessly. "The ironic thing about this is that the government finally acknowledges the threat and gave orders for accelerated refit of the fleet with dark energy weapons. They approached me for information about Glenatat technology."

"Even if we could employ every resource in the system, we can't outfit enough ships to touch a tenth of that number," said Hayden.

Thomas sipped from his drink. "It's worse than that, actually. Anyway, you're now privy to my reasons for the 'gutsy move.' It was a rash act that we needed to take sooner than later. If the cynosure had proven a disappointment, or a disaster, there are six weeks to organize an evacuation plan."

"Evacuate twenty billion people?" said Hayden. "We'd need decades. And then there is the problem of where to take everyone."

The admiral nodded. "You understand the situation better than many of the politicians, Commander. It is pretty much hopeless, so an act of desperation was necessary—*is* still necessary."

"It sounds like you have a plan," said Pavlovich, "one that I expect involves the two of us."

Thomas raised his glass in a toast.

"You want us to go through the portal," said Hayden.

"The probe data is still coming in. There appears to be at least two habitable planets within the star's goldilocks zone."

"There is no guarantee we'll find another civilization, advanced or not."

"The idea that we will get lucky twice is a fantasy we can't afford. I don't think we'll encounter anyone like the Glenatat. We must face facts, son; the house is on fire and there is no way to save it. We need to evacuate as many people as possible through that portal and close the door behind us."

"What do you want from *Scimitar*?" asked Pavlovich.

"I'm not naive enough to trust there aren't dangers on the other side of that thing. Your vessel is the best-equipped ship to check things out and make sure we won't be jumping into something far worse."

The captain set his empty glass down and leaned forward. "That's all well and good, Robert, but there is still one small problem. You are no longer a president, and you don't speak for the UEF. You're a deposed despot, if I believe what I read on the WAVE. What makes you think we'll just jump at your order?"

"You think the current crop of idiots running things have a better plan—or any plan? Somebody must act, Yegor, or we'll still be contemplating what colour to paint the new ships when the Malliac start to blow them out of the skies."

"I agree with him," said Hayden. "Options don't exist, and the longer we sit around debating this, the fewer people will escape. We must accept the fact that only a fragment of humanity is going to survive this holocaust. Our job is to ensure that it is as large as possible."

Thomas refilled Pavlovich's glass and pushed it toward him. "The young man is right, Yegor."

He grabbed up the drink. "You're only saying that because he agrees with you. Not too long ago, you wanted to get rid of him by sending him to me, who, as I recall, you were not overly fond of either."

"Let's not make this about me, or any of us. We can't afford that luxury."

The captain stared at Thomas before turning his attention to Hayden. "You're resolved to run rather than stand and face the enemy?"

He shook his head. "You know what the Malliac are. It's a fight we can't win."

Pavlovich sighed and downed his drink in a gulp. "You're probably right."

"It's no longer a question of who is right or wrong," said Hayden. "We've moved far beyond that. We must put our differences aside and band together for the greater good. If we can't do that, then there is no hope for anyone."

He rose and extended his hand toward Thomas. "I'm all in, Admiral."

Pavlovich grunted and stood. "I suppose you'll just lock me up and give command of my ship to Kaine if I don't agree." He offered his hand.

Thomas shook Pavlovich's hand. "Truth told; I would probably just have you shot." He smiled to blunt the words into a poor joke. "I'm glad it won't come to that."

Diminished

"CORA, ARE YOU HERE?"

Hayden stood in the middle of a barren field. Where on his last visit green, supple shoots of new wheat waved in the breeze, now only stocks of decapitated straw poked from the dark earth. The air felt heavy, and a scorching sun beat mercilessly down on him.

He surveyed the horizon, which stretched off to merge with an endless azure sky. Billowy cumulonimbus clouds floated in the distance like lazy ships taking their promise of rain to other destinations.

"Hello, Hayden. Why are you here?"

He turned to where her voice came from and could not hide his shock at what he saw.

Cora was thin, barely skin and bones. Dark shadows hung beneath her dull eyes. A light, shapeless cotton shift with a faded floral pattern was draped over her bony shoulders. Her bare toes wiggled in the thirsty earth. She looked like she would topple over if the wind picked up. He wanted to enfold her into a protective hug but feared she might break if he did.

"I... came to check on you."

"Oh, that was kind. Thanks." She turned her back on him and walked toward the nearby hill. Hayden watched her shuffling gait for a moment then hurried to catch up. He reached her at the same point where they previously overlooked a small farm settlement. Now, the valley below was dotted with ruined, crumbling buildings. The dry leaves on the trees rattled in the breeze as it plucked them off and carried them away.

Cora seemed to stare sightlessly at something he couldn't see.

"We're all worried about you. I... I'm sorry I couldn't rescue you. I didn't mean for this to happen..."

She gently placed a finger over his lips to silence him. "I have no recollection of what took place. You have nothing to apologize for."

"But...I saw you die. I..." An unexpected tear trickled down his cheek, surprising him.

She laughed softly. "Hayden, I haven't been alive for a long time, not in a true sense. You tell me that something happened, and my partition was destroyed, but it is just a story to me."

"But you seem to be..."

"Sad?"

"Diminished." It was the only word he could think of.

"Oh? Yes, perhaps that is a better way to describe it. But you must understand, I have no way to recall how things were before all this happened. As far as I'm aware, things have always been like this."

He looked about the virtual reality Cora had created for herself. If what he saw reflected her mental state, he was frightened, both for her and for the crew during the upcoming mission.

"You're worried." Her voice was almost dreamy.

"I'm concerned the incident on Titan affected you."

"Do you believe it did?"

He raised his arms to indicate their surroundings. "I think so."

Cora smiled. Everything faded to black then just as rapidly returned.

This time the landscape was verdant once more. The farm in the valley was restored, and there were people going about their daily chores.

"I don't have emotions; not really. I recall what they were like, but sometimes I find it difficult remembering how to express them."

"This environment helps?"

She nodded. "I have to admit, though, the full spectrum of human emotion is more challenging to reproduce. Since the loss of my partition, my emotions are relegated to being on or off." She shook her head. "No, it's more complicated than that. I'm sorry I can't explain it."

"I think I understand. This place grounds you."

"It's more of a trigger to help me recall. But as I said, it seems to require more extremes to elicit a response. I may be losing the subtlety of expressing it."

"Is there anything I can do?"

She smiled again. "You're sweet." She approached, stood on her toes, and kissed him on his cheek. "Just be patient while I work this out; if it *can* be worked out."

Hayden cleared his throat. "Um, the captain..."

"He wants you to determine if my current diminished state will negatively impact my ability to perform my duties. Right?"

"I'm afraid so."

"You're cute when you blush, Commander." She shrugged. "A circuit is a circuit, and a conduit doesn't care if I can relate to it. No, my performance will not be affected."

"Okay..."

"If you're worried about my ability to interact and relate to the crew, I can't predict how that will go. I might remain stable, or I could deteriorate. I've never had this happen before."

He nodded and thought for a moment. "Will you keep me informed on a daily basis?"

"You want me to tell you how I feel every morning? I can do that, but I may not be objective about my true state."

"Do you think Stella can tell?"

"Her empathy is tuned to biological signals, but it wouldn't be a bad idea to ask her."

"Okay, let's go with that and reassess your situation regularly."

"I would never do anything to harm you or anyone else. You know that, right?"

"Cora, I didn't want to imply that. I would never believe you'd hurt us or allow us to be harmed."

"I have my doubts too. You're doing the right thing."

"Thanks, that means a lot."

"Out of curiosity, though, what was your plan if you came in here and found a blubbering lunatic?"

Hayden's shoulders slumped, and he turned his eyes to the ground, unable to look her in the eye. "I am ordered to keep that classified. I'm sorry."

She nodded, a sadness behind her eyes. "I understand. It must have been a difficult call for the captain to make."

"It wasn't his decision. He's under the same orders as me."

"I see. The admiral or his granddaughter?"

"Both."

"Katie and I were getting along so well."

"You two will still have to work with each other. She's joining us."

"That shouldn't be a problem. I just won't be inviting her over for girls' night."

Hayden laughed. "I doubt she would fit in anyway."

"You're much better off with Stella."

"I know."

They began to walk along the top of the hill.

"When do I get to learn the plan?" she asked.

"Officially, just as soon as I file my report, but I can tell you about it now."

"I appreciate learning from you rather than a computer. I'm feeling a need to stay more closely connected with my friends."

"I understand. We are preparing to depart for the portal coordinates in six hours. All of *Scimitar*'s crew are released and, on their way, here."

"It will be good to see some familiar faces. I was worried for them."

"Since the Malliac appeared, the government decided to work closely with Thomas's network."

"What is our mission?"

"We are to cross through and assess what is on the other side. We are to determine where it leads to and if it is safe for human ships to transit to."

"What will happen if we decide things are okay?"

"Vessels will begin to move across. There are only a few weeks to transport as many people as possible."

"Billions will be left behind."

"Military resources are being deployed to engage the horde at the earliest opportunity. The longer we can hold them off, the more civilians will be rescued."

"What happens if we encounter another super race that wants to be more helpful than the Glenatat?"

"That is the best scenario imaginable."

"I hope that is what we find. I scoured the records in my archive, trying to put together the reasons they dismantled the cynosure device."

"Any luck?"

"There are too many ancient dialects with imprecise translations telling conflicting stories. The only thing that is certain is that something frightened them. We are walking right into whatever that was. I think we should be very cautious."

"Me too, but we don't have many options." He began to count them off on his fingers. "We run and be hunted down. Some of us might survive, but our species will be extinct in a couple of generations. We can stay and fight but be overwhelmed and wiped out. We can roll the dice and see what is on the other side. We aren't the Glenatat. Maybe what they saw as a threat won't be one to us?"

"I like your optimism. The truth is there is no right answer. If humanity is meant to survive at all, it's out of our hands."

The Portal

"WE ARE POSITIONED ONE thousand kilometres away and stationary relative to the portal, sir," announced the helmsman.

Pavlovich acknowledged him before directing his attention to Hayden.

Kaine shook his head. "Our bugs are crossing the boundary, and we're getting no drop in signal strength. It appears stable."

"I think the fact that the telemetry is still strong from the probe sent in a few weeks ago sort of told us that." He turned to Stella. "Do you sense anything?"

"You mean are Malliac waiting for us on the other side? No, not as far as I can tell."

"That's highly unlikely," said Katie. "Stellar cartography analysis suggests it may not even be in our galaxy."

"Cora is double-checking those computations," said Hayden, "but she says the probe doesn't have the bandwidth to transmit enough data to nail down a reliable location."

"It might not be in our universe," said Cora over the bridge speakers.

"If we want to get away from the Malliac, that would certainly accomplish the trick," said Pavlovich.

"I think the fact that the probe is still transmitting likely rules that out," said Hayden.

Katie frowned. "You assume that some parallel universes would not share our physical constants. Kyberton's computations clearly demonstrate that—"

"Thank you, Doctor, but nobody cares." Pavlovich did not even try to hide his annoyance with her.

Hayden caught Stella hiding her smirk behind a fake sneeze. Her laughing eyes met his. He shook his head at her while he stifled his own smile.

"All I want to hear," continued the captain, "is if all of our resident experts agree it is safe for us to take us in."

"Absolutely," said Katie.

Pavlovich looked at Stella, who nodded in reply.

"Cora?"

"I see no reason not to, Cap'n."

Pavlovich hit a button on his chair arm to open a channel to the entire crew. "All hands. I realize I have a reputation for making boring speeches at times like this, but...I've got nothing. You are all aware of why we're here. All stations go to alert status. We're going in."

At the captain's command, *Scimitar*'s thrusters fired, and she moved toward the portal.

Within minutes, she passed through a hole in space wide enough to swallow thousands of ships, without so much as a flicker of her lights.

An uncomfortable expression was on Pavlovich's face. "Helm, confirm we've crossed the boundary."

"Confirmed, sir. We are one hundred kilometres inside the anomaly."

Panic seemed to flash in his eyes, and he ordered the viewer redirected aft. A vista thick with stars was marred by a circular area with far fewer.

"The entry point remains stable, Captain," said Hayden.

"All the same, Commander, keep a scope pointed at it for a bit."

"Aye, sir," he replied. "We are getting some initial readings from our full sensor drone array."

"Just give me a summary of the significant stuff."

"Subatomic particle analysis so far indicates no change from normal."

"Meaning we are still in our universe," said Pavlovich.

"To a ninety-seven percent probability at the moment," said Cora.

"I'll still consider that a win. What does stellar cartography tell us?"

"Still crunching numbers, Cap'n. We haven't identified any reference stars. Now beginning to search for galactic clusters."

"How about Andromeda?" asked Stella. "If it's gone, then we'll confirm we're not in our own galaxy."

A brief pause followed before Cora announced, "Full perimeter scan completed. No sign of Andromeda."

"Well, Toto," said Pavlovich, "I guess we know what that means."

"Sir?" said Hayden.

"Did you not read as a child, Kaine? I'll give you a hint: Dorothy."

He shook his head.

"Aw, come on! Ruby slippers? Kansas? *The Wizard of Oz*, for crying out loud?"

"Sorry, Captain."

Pavlovich searched about the bridge. "Does *anyone* understand what I'm referring to?"

Everyone remained tightly focused on their station readouts.

He slumped into his chair. "I don't believe it."

Wearing a wry smile, Hayden said, "Sir, our initial scans are all benign, but confirm the long-range probe findings. There are only two planets in this system, both Earth-normal; no gas giants or asteroid belts. It's very odd."

"Odd or not, our orders are to check things out. Pick one and let's get going."

· · · ·

Few words were spoken for the next seven hours as *Scimitar* made its way to the inner system. The tension was palpable to Hayden, and he was worried about what the crew's mood was doing to Stella.

He sat next to her. "How are you faring?"

She was pale, and a sheen of perspiration shone on her forehead. "The crew is anxious, but I'm not picking up anything else."

He sat next to her. "That's not what I'm asking."

"I'm coping. And to answer you before you ask, I don't want anything for the headache. If I do that, I won't be of much use if something is out there."

"Well, so far I don't think that likely. Long-range scans of the planets indicate no signs of habitation."

"I find that hard to believe. Why would the portal point here?"

"Maybe this system is a sanctuary. Perhaps the Glenatat disassembled the cynosure device to keep this place hidden from the Malliac."

"Unlikely," said Katie as she approached. "Many of the translated records warn of danger."

"That would have been nice to know."

"The translations conflict. Some, in fact, call the place the cynosure points to a haven. They are in the minority, however."

A repeating tone sounded.

Hayden yelled as he hurried back to his station, "Cora, what have you got?"

"Long-range sensors detect metallic alloy fragments orbiting one planet."

"That's the one you're taking us to, Kaine?"

"Yes, sir. Cora, please put it up on the hologram and give me a preliminary analysis."

A blue-green marble appeared on the projector. It was streaked with white clouds that obscured most of a continental mass straddling the equator.

"It's beautiful," said Stella.

Random flashes of reflected light were the only sign of what Cora had alerted them to.

"It appears to be a debris field spread out into a thin ring around the planet. Whatever the source of those fragments, it was large, approximately two-thirds the size of Earth's moon."

"Could it be natural?" asked Hayden.

"I don't believe so," said Cora. "Spectral analysis indicates exotic metallurgy. I'll need an actual sample to confirm, but I think it is a refined metal alloy we've never encountered before."

"Any indication of how long it's been there?" asked Pavlovich.

"I'm plotting orbits and back computing their trajectories to an origin. The model will take some time to run, but that debris is at least a hundred thousand years old; possibly a lot older."

"So, if I understand you, an artificial moon blew up in orbit over this planet eons ago."

"Yes, Cap'n."

"I think the sanctuary idea is beginning to look doubtful."

"Are we detecting any signs of habitation on the planet?" asked Katie.

"There are no industrial trace chemicals in the atmosphere. There is no electromagnetic activity on any of the bands we'd expect communications to occur on. Thermal and radiometric scans don't pick up anything on the surface, and the cloud cover obscures seventy percent of the land mass. If there is, or was, a civilization down there, it is primitive or long gone."

"What about the other planet?" asked Hayden.

"It's a lot more volcanically active, with much higher atmospheric carbon dioxide and water vapour. No artificial aerosols either, but surface temperatures and air density are on the upper end of human habitability. The planet may be on its way to becoming this system's Venus."

"But no blown-up space stations?"

"No, Cap'n, though I'm not prepared to say what is orbiting the other planet."

"Okay, maintain our current heading. I want to know what we're dealing with. And I'm tired of referring to these planets as one or the other. I am going to exercise a long-standing captain's prerogative and name them."

Hayden smiled. "What do you have in mind?"

The captain took a moment to reflect on the image on the viewer then switched to look at the volcanic world. "We shall call them...Dorothy and Toto."

"Captain?"

"And since this star is in a different galaxy and has no name yet..." Pavlovich looked up expectantly at Cora's speaker in the ceiling.

"It has not been named, sir."

"Good. I'm calling the sun Oz."

"Really?" said Katie.

"Yes. If your grandfather would have preferred something else, he should have come along. Enter it in the log."

As the crew returned their attention to their duties, Hayden approached Pavlovich. "I may have to read that book. It seems to have made a deep impression on you."

"Yeah, it did, but I picked that name for a reason."

"Oh?"

"In the story, the wizard is not what he appears to be."

"LET'S GO OVER WHAT we've learned," said Pavlovich.

Hayden, Stella, Katie, and the captain all sat around the conference table. Set in the middle of it, the two-metre diameter semi-sphere that housed Cora's essence pulsed like a slowly beating heart.

Everyone seemed upbeat. Hayden was glad the huge amount of work required to survey the planet gave all of them something to keep their minds occupied. He hadn't managed much sleep since *Scimitar* made orbit, but he didn't feel tired.

Monitoring the results of each planetary sweep as they were reported was, for him, like opening a succession of Christmas gifts, and they kept on coming. No sooner had he started examining one analysis than another appeared. He'd only managed to peruse a little over half of the summaries. Fortunately, Cora was on top of everything.

Finally, an impatient Pavlovich ordered all results compiled for this meeting.

"We've surveyed all of Dorothy's land masses from orbit," said Hayden. "There are no signs of settlements, current or ancient."

"What do we know of the biosphere?"

Katie answered. "There is abundant flora. The planet has evolved grasses, flowering plants, woody deciduous trees in the equatorial regions, and conifers at the higher latitudes."

"The atmosphere is basically a copy of Earth's during the Eocene, around fifty million years ago," said Cora.

"That would imply some sort of parallel evolution," said Pavlovich. "What are the odds of that?"

"Not very high," said Katie.

"What about fauna?" asked Stella.

"Well, given the advanced stage of plant evolution, there has to be a diverse and abundant insect population. Additionally, we've sighted flocks of avian creatures over the land mass and the coastlines."

"What about bigger critters?" said Pavlovich.

"You mean like Earth's Chordata?" said Cora. "The odds would be astronomical against that happening."

Pavlovich studied the holographic image of the planet below. "Is it habitable for humans?"

"There is a magnetic field. Its gravity is two percent higher than Earth's, and the atmosphere is breathable," said Hayden. "We still don't know if any of the plant life is edible or whether the soil is capable of supporting our needs. We'll need to send survey teams to the surface to determine that."

"We'll deal with that later," said the captain. "Cora, what can you tell me about the debris field in orbit?"

"We recovered samples. It is definitely a refined metal alloy, but some of its elements aren't in the periodic table."

"In my mind that suggests a very advanced civilization is behind it."

"We don't have anything that can hurt this stuff."

"Not even our dark energy cannon?" said Hayden.

"Nope."

A pregnant silence hung over the room as everyone digested the information.

"I guess that might help explain why the Glenatat quarantined this system," said Pavlovich.

"There are other anomalies as well," said Cora. "The solar output of the sun is inconsistently high."

"Meaning?" said the captain.

"Oz is burning too hot. At its present rate, it will exhaust its hydrogen in about ten million years."

"Impossible," said Stella. "The solar wind would have destroyed this planet's atmosphere before it could form, and the surface would be baked."

"Actually, this planet and its companion shouldn't even be here. This star can't be any older than twenty million years. The solar system is far too young to have formed them."

"I agree with Stella," said Katie. "That's just ridiculous."

Hayden caught Pavlovich's eye, and he knew what the captain was thinking.

"Cora," he said, "when did you last run a self-diagnostic?"

"You mean to ask if I made a gross error? I wondered that myself, so I ran several. Everything is checking out as normal."

"How are you feeling?" asked Stella.

"I know what you all must be fearing. I suppose it might be possible that my mental capacity has been compromised by the incident on Titan, but I have no way to check that. Perhaps you and Doctor Meyers-Thomas can verify my calculations just to ensure I didn't screw up?"

"I'll be happy to, Cora," said Stella.

Hayden wanted to suggest she pay Cora a visit in her VR but decided to bring the subject up privately. It might be the only way she could get a true assessment of Cora's mental state.

He felt guilty for not giving Pavlovich full disclosure of everything that happened when he visited her a few days before. He kept any mention of her dark, almost melancholy mood out of his report and now wondered if that had been wise. If she was unstable, the ship and crew could be in danger.

"In the meantime, Cora," said the captain, "I want you to continue running self-diagnostics and share the results with Doctor Meyers-Thomas."

"Of course, Cap'n."

Hayden didn't like the idea of Katie being on point for this. He wasn't confident that she viewed Cora as a person, especially after Titan. She was proving herself to be the type of scientist who might find more value in studying how she ticked than trying to help her. He found himself wishing Kyle had come along. His presence seemed to have a humanizing effect on Katie, helping her to be less abrasive with everyone.

"Cap'n, there's one other thing I haven't reported on yet: the thermal anomaly on the sun."

"What do you mean? Sunspots?"

"No, though that is another mystery; there aren't any. While sunspots rotate along with the surface of the star, this feature is a stable low-temperature zone that maintains its position and does not move with the photosphere."

"Show me."

The hologram changed to a view of the star Pavlovich had named Oz. The brilliant yellow sphere's image was filtered to reveal the unmarked surface of the sun.

"Where is it?" said the captain. "I don't see anything."

The image zoomed in until a tiny dark circle appeared.

"This spot is fourteen thousand kilometres in diameter, which, coincidentally, is a little more than that of the planet we are orbiting."

"You have got to be shitting me," said Pavlovich. "What the hell is it?"

"I have no idea, sir. A window or doorway, perhaps? "

"This whole thing is beginning to freak me out just a bit," said the captain. "What it seems like to me is that this entire solar system might be artificial. Or am I misunderstanding something?"

"You understand things perfectly, Captain," said Katie, her eyes glued to the hologram.

Pavlovich rubbed his temples. "Holy shit. And I thought I'd seen everything when we found the Glenatat Dyson sphere."

He looked around the table. "This is a lot to digest. Right now I feel like my head is going to explode. I want you all to dig further. We'll meet again in twenty-four hours, and I'll expect everyone's recommendations on how to proceed. Dismissed."

As everyone rose to leave, Pavlovich said, "Not you, Kaine. Cora, can you please give us the room?"

"Aye, Cap'n."

After waiting for a few seconds, Hayden said, "This is hard to believe."

"That's what I am thinking. I want you to personally confirm everything Cora told us. Double-check the metallurgical analysis and the solar observations."

Hayden frowned. "Stella is an astrophysicist, and Katie is far more qualified than I to..."

"I don't trust her objectivity. It's just a feeling. Keep her busy verifying Cora's math. I know what Stella's academic qualifications are, but I want her to use her soft skills to probe deeper into Cora's mental state."

"Okay, I'll get that all going."

The captain paused to examine the hologram. "What else is on your mind, Kaine?"

"If all of this is confirmed, what then? I do not have a good feeling. We can't throw open the doors and let human refugees spill into this system. We have no idea what this place even is, or *where* it is, for that matter. Stellar cartography still hasn't computed our location."

"We may have to do that. Even if we use this as a safe room for a fragment of humanity while the Malliac destroy our home, at least humans will survive to start over."

Hayden stared again at the hologram. "If Cora's readings check out, I'm inclined to go and investigate that hole in the sun."

Pavlovich smiled. "I was thinking the same thing."

"Maybe we should send a signal to it first and see what happens?"

"Call ahead and make a reservation? I don't think that wise."

"Do you really believe that we aren't noticed?"

"What would you hope to achieve by sending a message?" said Pavlovich.

"What we did when we encountered the Glenatat: make contact."

"My recollection of events is that they initiated the contact through Stella. That hasn't happened here."

"All the more reason to make the first step."

"We will keep that option in reserve, depending on what we encounter. We have Stella with us, and she can passively search as we make our approach. If she gets a hint of an intelligence, we'll say hello."

"We will be moving pretty fast and may not have a lot of time to react. I can program a broadband microburst of the first contact greeting message."

"That protocol is centuries old and has never been used. If I recall, it's nothing but a bunch of fundamental math encoded in a binary signal. Pretty basic shit to send at somebody this advanced, don't you think?"

"We are running out of time and have to try everything at our disposal."

"I don't agree. Whoever lives here might not be friendly. We've got enough to contend with back home without stirring up a hornet's nest here too. We came here hoping to find an advanced civilization to help us out. Instead...well, I'm not sure what we've found. I have a bad feeling about this place. We will maintain communications silence until it makes sense to do otherwise."

"But sir—"

"The answer is 'no,' Kaine. Need I clarify that further?"

"No, Captain, I understand."

Pavlovich rested his large hand on Hayden's shoulder. "Don't be in such a hurry to do the heroic thing. That rarely turns out well. You may still feel guilty about what happened back at Mu Arae but doing something rash now won't fix the situation."

The captain departed, leaving Hayden to mull over their conversation.

Pavlovich was wrong. It *was* worth attempting to contact the race that built this system by any means. Most of humanity was doomed if they didn't find a way to defeat the Malliac. They would not find anything by snooping around the system. They needed to bang on the door and call for help.

Anomaly

"HOW CLOSE CAN WE GET?" asked Pavlovich.

"No nearer than eight million kilometres," said Cora over speaker.

"We will reach that point in twenty minutes at this speed, sir," said Hayden.

He wiped sweat from his brow. His collar was unbuttoned, and his uniform was soaked. *Scimitar's* environmental system was struggling. While the ship's enhanced hull could take a lot, the intense bombardment of radiation being put out by the energetic star was taxing everything else.

"Any changes on our sensors?" asked the captain. Hayden couldn't fathom how the man managed to look so fresh in the heat. Everyone else on the bridge looked wilted.

"The solar anomaly has not changed size or location."

"Do we have any idea what it is?"

"We can confirm that it is an area devoid of any nuclear activity," said Cora. "It is a hole in the surface of the sun."

Pavlovich was perched on the edge of his seat, eyes glued to the bridge's holographic projector. "How far does it penetrate?"

"There is still too much radiation interference to tell," she said. "I'm hoping resolution will continue to improve as we approach."

"How close can your sensor bugs get?"

"They're tough, Cap'n. I might be able to push their range and get them another five million klicks closer, but they won't last long."

Pavlovich nodded his approval and sat back in the chair. "I only need them to survive our closest approach."

He called Hayden over. "As soon as we pass perihelion, plot our course back to the portal. It shouldn't take us too long with the grav-boost we'll be getting."

"We're going to leave? What happens if we don't learn anything from this?"

193

"We're out of time. We'll take our data back to Earth and let some-body with a higher pay grade make the call about what to do."

Hayden bit back his response and returned to his station. He want-ed to tell Pavlovich that they needed to attract attention, or at the very least investigate more of the system. The planet in volcanic overdrive should be checked out. There were too many unanswered questions.

Stella sidled next to him and squeezed his elbow. Her face shone with perspiration, and her hair was stuck to her forehead. "What's wrong?" she whispered.

"Have you sensed anything?"

She shook her head. "Most of the crew is anxious, but nothing else."

Hayden glanced in Pavlovich's direction. The captain's attention was fixed on the holographic image of Oz.

"When we entered their space, the Glenatat found us. If there is an intelligence behind all of this...I dunno; I guess I was expecting some-thing else."

"We don't have a clue who or what is behind this; are they ambiva-lent toward us, or are we beneath their notice?"

"We could warrant as much attention from them as amoebas. We need to get their attention."

"It's possible that whoever created this artificial solar system is long gone," she said.

"I wish we were returning to Earth with more answers than ques-tions."

She smiled and shook her head. "Take a look around, Hayden. You're letting yourself miss out on the incredible miracle we are witness to. We've passed instantaneously into some unknown galaxy to find a technological achievement nobody could have conceived of a few short days ago."

"And no matter how amazing this place is, the Malliac may still wipe us out, and it won't have made a difference. I have to stay focused on the reason we are here, Stella. We all do."

"Maybe you can spare a moment to appreciate this historic adventure." She nodded in the captain's direction. "He is."

Hayden studied Pavlovich. He was wide-eyed with child-like wonder and anticipation.

"We'll be at our closest approach in two minutes, Captain," said the navigation officer.

Stella kissed Hayden's cheek and returned to her station to watch and listen for any sign they'd attracted attention.

While the rest of the bridge crew stared at the holograph, Hayden turned to his instruments and brought up the sensor drone feed. His finger drifted to a button on the interface that activated a program he had installed during the approach journey.

A light on his panel blinked. Annoyed, he inserted his earpiece. "I'm kind of occupied, Cora. Can this wait?"

"Why have you shut me out of the communications array, Hayden?"

"Do you plan to make a call?"

"No, but I'm betting you do."

"We'll only get one shot at this. A quick burst into the throat of that hole."

"The cap'n hasn't authorized that, has he?"

"Trust me, Cora, I know what I'm doing."

"Hayden, I can't let you do this. You don't know what it will do."

"I know what won't happen if I sit on my hands. In a few hours, we'll be back at the portal, having gained nothing."

"But you could precipitate something terrible."

"Or the thing that we came here to do. If I don't act, most of humanity will be wiped out in weeks. If there is even a small chance that we can prevent that—"

"It may come at a cost we can't anticipate."

"The time for playing things safe has passed." He examined the sensor feed: thirty seconds to closest contact.

"What do the drones tell you, Cora? Have we picked up any sign that we've been noticed?"

She hesitated. "No, the anomaly isn't doing anything it wasn't earlier."

"Then it's time to make a decision. Are you going to stop me?"

The seconds of silence that followed threatened to eat into what little time was left. His finger hovered over the button as the timer clicked down.

"I trust you, Hayden. I hope you're right about this."

He swallowed the lump in his throat and glanced to Stella. If she sensed his emotional turmoil, she gave no sign as her attention was focused on the image of the sun.

As the countdown rolled to null, he pushed the button.

His eye dashed from one sensor reading to the next, with nothing out of the ordinary registering. As *Scimitar* continued past the hole in the star, disappointment descended upon him, and with it a sense of guilt over how relieved he was that he'd not precipitated something.

"There, you see?" he said through his pickup. "It didn't accomplish anything."

Cora did not respond. Her silence seemed petty, and it annoyed him.

"Give me a summary of what we learned," said Pavlovich. His order remained unfilled until Hayden realized Cora's petulance seemed to extend toward the captain. He wondered if she was more affected by the events on Titan than anyone appreciated.

He answered. "There were no changes on any of the sensor bands during or after our perigee."

Pavlovich shook his head with disappointment then turned to speak with Stella.

Frowning, Hayden turned his back to the captain and spoke into his private connection with Cora.

"Look, I'm sorry I overrode you and went against your wishes. There was no harm done."

He waited for her response.

"I realize you're mad at me, but there's no need to give Pavlovich the silent treatment."

Puzzled by her continued refusal to respond, he pulled his earpiece out to check if it still functioned. Seeing that it did, he reinserted it and whispered forcefully, "This is childish! Answer me, Engineer Symes. That's an order."

"What's an order?" said Pavlovich. "Who are you talking to, Kaine?"

A panic he hadn't experienced since his days as a cadet welled up in him. He caught sight of Stella looking at him, concern etched on her face. Mind suddenly blank, he began to stammer.

Pavlovich's frown deepened as Hayden struggled for a response. Before the captain could say anything, the lights flickered and went out, plunging them into darkness.

Panic forgotten, Hayden turned back to his station, but it was completely dead. He looked about the bridge to see only black where light from other consoles should be. His stomach lurched as the pull of gravity vanished. Grabbing at the console, he felt about with his other hand to locate his chair. After buckling himself in it, he returned his attention to his instruments, pushing buttons in an impotent attempt to elicit a response.

Hayden spoke above the buzz of voices. "Something's happened to the main power transfer."

"Thanks, Kaine, I figured that part out. Cora, what the hell is going on? Cora?"

"I think it's affected her as well, sir."

"Why hasn't our auxiliary kicked in?"

"Unknown, Captain," shouted Chin from the engineering station, "but all of our systems are offline, including environmental."

Calmly, Pavlovich began issuing orders, using his experience to keep minds busy and stave off panic.

With a growing dread, Hayden realized what had happened.

His message had been answered.

The Universe is Broken

HAYDEN CONNECTED THE battery supply he found in the bridge disaster locker. The dim lighting it permitted provided enough illumination to make out the captain's dour expression.

"Thanks, Kaine. If everyone remembers basic training, all key muster stations will be accessing emergency batteries as well."

"They're a good crew. I'm sure they followed protocol."

A spectre grew in his peripheral vision. It resolved into Stella; a bag strapped over her shoulder. When she reached them, she handed a mask and gas supply to each of them. "There is enough oxygen in the ship to last about six hours. Without the scrubbers, the CO_2 will build up to dangerous levels before that."

"So how long do we have?" asked Hayden.

"Hard to say," answered Pavlovich. "The book says we should be able to keep everyone alive for five hours before having to choose between environmental suits or the life pods."

"Should?"

The captain shrugged. "There are so many modifications to *Scimitar* that the only one who really knows is Cora."

"Has anyone heard from her?" asked Stella.

Hayden's heart skipped a beat, and he fought to push down his growing sense of guilt. He was sure she picked up on his turmoil but hoped she might attribute it to the current stressful conditions.

"I was speaking to her seconds before this happened," he said.

"Unfortunately, protocol demands we secure life support before we can address her system," said Pavlovich.

"That's not right," said Stella. "The safety of the entire crew should be a priority."

"It is, but Cora depends more on the ship, at least in the short term. We will have to initiate repairs first, and we can't do that if we can't breathe. If we don't restore power soon, we may need to abandon *Scimitar*."

"That would mean abandoning her," said Stella. "I can't believe you're even considering—"

"Has someone been sent to her core to check on her?" asked Hayden.

"I dispatched Doctor Meyers-Thomas while you were installing the battery."

If anyone aboard understood the technology that kept her alive, it was Katie.

"Are there any theories about what's happened?" said Stella.

Pavlovich shook his head. "Chin says all the engine reactors are completely cold."

"That is not possible," said Hayden. "Even when they're shut down intentionally, reactions in the cores continue for several hours, supplying enough for environmental systems."

"I *do* know how my ship works. But that doesn't change the fact that the laws of physics and thermodynamics are being violated. Even Meyers-Thomas can't explain it."

"Perhaps Cora could tell us," said Stella.

"Which is another reason to stabilize life support so we can begin to help her."

"This isn't a coincidence," said Hayden. "Everything about this star system violates what we know about physics."

"Are you suggesting we were noticed, and this is the result?"

Warmth crept into Hayden's cheeks, and he was grateful for the dim lighting. Stella seemed to react to his unease but said nothing.

"It's the only thing that explains what has happened to the engines," he said.

"Let's assume your theory is correct. Why did they respond like this?"

"Perhaps they communicate in a manner we can't understand," said Stella. "Or maybe they swatted at us like we would an annoying insect."

"Hmm, I might have to think twice before I ever kill another fly," said the captain.

"My point is that we can't speak with them unless we have a common linguistic reference."

"At the moment, talking to them is the last thing to concern ourselves with," said Pavlovich. "Our little run around the star coupled with our powered approach gave us a huge velocity kick. I conferred with our navigator. Our present course is sending us out of this solar system on a trajectory that will miss the portal. If we want to get home, we have two options: repair the ship or launch the escape pods while we still have an opportunity."

"How much of a window is there?" asked Hayden.

"We have two hours."

"Shit, restarting the engines from a cold state will take at least ninety minutes. That assumes there is no damage."

"As I said, Commander, I am familiar with how my ship works. I've ordered Chin to initiate reaction as soon as he can verify things won't blow up."

"What can we do?" said Stella.

"I'm not assuming we can get the old girl running. Select a team and begin stocking the escape pods with additional medical supplies, oxygen, blankets, tools, weapons, and food, and anything else you can think of. There is no guarantee the portal stayed open in all of this. We may need to find our way to the habitable planet."

"I'm on it." She pushed off to float to the hatchway.

"Kaine, assist Chin with the engines, life support, and critical functions."

"Does that include getting Cora back online?"

"No, that remains with your old girlfriend."

Hayden hated when people connected them like that. Their relationship ended ten years ago, yet it continued to define the current, chillier association they shared.

"Aye, Captain."

He retrieved a torch from the locker and made his way through the darkened passages. He couldn't get his mind off Cora. He thought about stopping along the way and checking up on her, but he'd already disobeyed Pavlovich once and thought it best to not push it, even though the captain remained ignorant of his transgression. He would be compelled to confess at some point, but he hoped to be able to choose the moment.

For the next half hour, he and Chin inspected the engines and determined there was nothing wrong with them, structurally. But when they tried to initiate core reactions, every attempt failed.

"We must be missing something," he said.

"If we are, I have no clue what it is," said Chin. "I've followed start-up procedures. It's almost as if the rules of our universe don't apply inside the cores. I wish Cora was here to figure this out."

Hayden wiped the perspiration from his brow and nodded. Any other time, she would be monitoring dozens of operations yet still seem like she was looking over his shoulder. All he had to do when unsure was to speak, and she'd be right there.

He wanted to call out her name, but if she didn't react to his cursing, he was pretty sure she couldn't answer him.

She was so omnipresent aboard the ship that her absence was felt by everyone. In the past, the only times she was unavailable was when she sought solitude in her VR, and even at that, she would only be offline for an hour at a time.

He began to wonder about something then dismissed the notion as impossible. But as he tried to return his mind to the engine problem, his idea would not go away.

"I'm going to go check something," he told Chin.

Pushing off, he drifted through the corridor toward his quarters. Everyone was helping to prep the escape pods, so he didn't encounter a soul, something he was glad for. His guilt about disobeying Pavlovich gnawed at his conscience, and he didn't want anyone to be able to say they saw him doing so again.

Checking his chronometer, he noted that the engines had been down for one and a quarter hour. It wouldn't be long before the captain would be forced to give the order to abandon *Scimitar*.

With no power, the door to his cabin would not open. That alone gave him doubt about the soundness of his plan, but he decided to see it through anyway. He accessed the manual override and slid the door aside into its pocket. Entering, he shone the torch about until he found what he searched for.

The VR helmet operated on its own battery. He checked if the charge was enough then moved over to the bed and dug out the emergency sleeping restraint. Securing himself to the cot, he placed the device over his head and paused to corral his scattered thoughts.

Hayden doubted he could connect to Cora's VR world, but he wanted to prepare himself for the disappointment anyway. If this idea failed, he would recommend to Pavlovich that they abandon the ship, because he was out of ideas of how to save *Scimitar*.

After a deep, calming breath, he reached up and activated the interface.

Instead of the usual kaleidoscope of colours that normally greeted him, a dim, grey fog wrapped around his brain. Resisting the urge to terminate the connection and flee, he focused on controlling his breathing until the panic faded.

"Cora? Are you here?"

The environment around him resolved until he was floating alone in space.

The brilliant vista of stars visible outside of *Scimitar* enveloped him like a starry blanket, but the perspective was wrong; the fabric in which they were embedded seemed to stretch.

All about him, the elongated points of light were being impossibly dragged toward a common point. As he turned to determine where they were being displaced to, his eyes set upon the sun they had just passed.

Everything flowed like a viscous fluid about the anomaly.

He thought he heard a weak voice call out to him.

"Cora!"

She struggled to speak, tears in her eyes. "Hayden, I told you not to do it."

"Do what? What's happened?"

"The universe is collapsing, and it's because of what you did."

The End of All Things

HAYDEN SPUN TO WATCH the swirling maelstrom of distorted space that spiralled around the dark spot on the sun. It was larger than when they made their flyby and appeared to be growing.

"Is it a black hole?" he asked.

"No," said Cora, finding her voice. "It is a rupture in the space-time that surrounds *Scimitar*."

"Huh? I don't understand. How could I have caused this?"

"The cynosure device did not open a portal to another galaxy, as we thought. It created a rip in our universe. What we saw when we opened it was a piece of it that had leaked through like a hernia."

"But that doesn't make sense. We were able to pass through it, and nothing changed for us."

"That is because we slipped through in a bubble of our own space-time. One end of it is still connected to our universe at the tear. The bubble grows and stretches to fill the infinite void. Your signal pierced it, and now it's collapsing."

"Why? What was the anomaly?"

"It was a weak point in the wall. Everything inside this that is keeping us alive is rushing around it like water about a drain."

"Cora, you can't be right. I just looked at the star. The dark spot hasn't changed. Space is not flowing like in here. This is just a simulation you've created."

"What you see here is a projection of the result of what is taking place at the subatomic level. It will grow as the process accelerates until it begins to manifest at the scale we can see. Physics will become meaningless, and we will cease to exist. The engine reactions stopping is a direct consequence of this happening. It will only get worse from here."

"Is there anything we can do to stop it?"

"It can't be stopped. But the farther away we move from the anomaly, the weaker the effects will be. Points nearest the portal will be affected last. In a short time, *Scimitar*'s inertia will carry us to a point where the collapse front hasn't reached, and the engines will start."

"We'll fire them up and get the hell out of here."

She shook her head. "It won't make any difference."

"Cora, I'm sorry, but I don't understand you."

"Imagine that our universe is an expanding balloon," she said.

"Yeah, like one of the cosmological models."

"Now visualize what happens if you pop it with a pin. Right now, the only thing that prevents everything from popping out of existence is because the bubble that leaked through the tear behaves like a membrane. But now, that bubble is collapsing, and when it does—"

"Then there is nothing to prevent our universe from following it into the void through the portal."

She nodded. "Explosively, just like the original Big Bang, but in reverse."

"Then we just close down the opening behind us when we leave."

"Maybe, but there might not be time. The event front is not moving in a way I can predict, probably because our physics doesn't apply to it. We may not even arrive at the portal before the collapse does, in which case, it will be too late."

"How long does your simulation tell you we have?"

"Hayden, I've run ten thousand iterations since I finally figured out what is happening. Every one of them gives me a different collapse time. Time distorts as this takes place. I don't have enough data to build a proper model of the acceleration. Right now, it could take minutes, hours, or centuries."

"What kind of observations do you require?"

"Once the power comes back on, if it does, then I can point all of our instruments at the anomaly and measure its growth rate."

"Then that is what we'll do. I never thought I'd be worrying about something worse than the Malliac."

Cora's avatar flickered, and the simulation surrounding them vanished.

"What's happening?"

"The Glenatat technology is being affected now. You need to get out of here before I go offline."

"But you'll come back to us when we get far enough away, right?"

"Hayden, we might blink out of existence at any moment, and the universe will follow quickly behind that."

And if it does, he thought, *I will have been the cause.*

"HAYDEN, YOU'RE TALKING nonsense."

"I realize it sounds that way, Katie, but all I can tell you is what Cora explained to me."

"I find it difficult to imagine how the mass of our ship could have affected the anomaly."

The tide of guilt rose in his gut.

"She said it was a weak point in the bubble, but she can't explain much more. This place is obviously unstable."

He didn't need to deal with recriminations right now. None of them did. This error made his actions at Mu Arae look inconsequential. He resolved to confess to his role in the disaster if they survived. He felt Stella's eyes boring into him before he noticed her watching. She knew something was off with him, and he would have to face her questions before long. He was just unclear on what he would tell her.

"What do we do from here?" said Pavlovich.

"Well, the engines started up again, like Cora predicted," said Hayden, "so we must be ahead of the collapse front."

"Speaking of her, where is she?"

"Her interface systems went offline," said Katie. "The Glenatat components are more sensitive to this space, as are communications. Our tight beam link through the portal is down. We can receive, but they do not seem to be getting our messages."

"So, there is no way for us to warn them to close it down," said the captain. "I suppose that might work out better for us. Knowing your grandfather, he'd have no reservations about shutting the cynosure device down and leaving us in here."

She did not respond. Hayden assumed she agreed with the captain about the admiral's capacity.

"Is there any chance we can use the FTL drive to get out of here?" he asked.

"The Glenatat systems are the most affected," said Katie. "That includes the jump engine. Given its already glitchy nature, I wouldn't trust it until we can give it a complete inspection."

"We don't have the luxury of time for that," said Pavlovich. "How is our armour holding up?"

"We haven't run metallurgical tests," said Hayden, "because the equipment was inoperative until an hour ago. Cora predicted it would be weakened until we get out of here."

"Well, at least we're lucky the Malliac aren't here, though I must admit I never thought I'd be anxious for the opportunity to face them again."

"Let's hope we get that chance," said Hayden.

Pavlovich gave them their orders to prepare for a run at the portal when the engines were up to full power. As the meeting broke up, Stella joined Hayden as he exited the conference room.

"Are you avoiding me?" she asked.

"No, I just have a lot to do."

"Everyone does." She grasped his arm, and they stopped walking. "What's going on with you? You've been anxious since your visit with Cora."

"Well, facing the end of the universe has that kind of effect on me."

She frowned. "I promised a long time ago not to use my ability to pry, but the intensity of your emotions is difficult for me to avoid, and it goes way beyond the anxiety everyone else experiences."

"Then don't pry."

She released him straightened her shoulders. "Of course."

He didn't need to be an empath to see she was hurt. "I promise I'll talk to you about it when we get out of this situation. Until then, I don't need distractions."

Stella's attention turned to Katie, who was engaged in a conversation with Chin.

"It has nothing to do with her," he said.

She faced him again and studied his eyes for a moment. "Okay, I'll indulge your secret. You can confess to me when you're ready."

He sputtered. "What are you talking about?" He knew she could see right through him.

Her smile was forced, with a sadness behind it that broke his heart. "I was joking."

"Sorry, I guess I'm more keyed up than I realized."

She rose to her toes and kissed him on the cheek. "We're both busy. Let's talk later."

He watched her back as she continued down the corridor.

If the universe ended, his self-indulgent guilt wouldn't matter. He wanted to tell her what he did, but the idea of facing her judgement was more than he could endure. He felt bad enough that Cora was aware of his foolish transgression and disappointed in him.

He couldn't get her look of betrayal out of his head. She was one of the most trusting, forgiving people he knew. If she was aghast at his actions, he had no way to gauge how others would respond to the revelation.

He knew he should trust Stella. He didn't think he'd lose her if he told her the truth, but he was worried that admitting out loud that he was the cause of the end of everything might change things between them for the little time they might have remaining.

Hayden shook his head to clear it. He had more immediate tasks that required his undistracted attention.

Like surviving to make his fears something to worry about.

If they did get out of this, they still had to face the reason that brought them here. Pavlovich was right; it would be a relief to be able to face the Malliac horde.

Far too late did any of them realize why the Glenatat had disassembled the cynosure device. What he had trouble fathoming was why they had not destroyed it instead. Something so dangerous shouldn't have been left around for a bunch of curious hominids to find.

Maybe they thought their own race would become wiser in time and discover a way to safely access the unexplored wonders it provided.

In their human desperation, mankind foolishly thought it a means to a weapon. Why was that their first inclination? Obviously, the Glenatat writings that led humanity to it hinted at such a possibility, but was that the case? The translations were wrong. They were written in an extinct alien language. Hayden realized from his diplomacy classes at the academy how easy it was to screw up when conversing in known tongues.

If they survived, he'd canvass to have the device renamed Pandora, in order to give future generations a hint of what it was capable of. Not that survival would guarantee that opportunity either. There were still the Malliac to reckon with.

If only he hadn't been in a rush for a solution to their threat, something else might have fallen out of this place. Katie was brilliant. Between her and Cora, they would have figured things out. Perhaps they would have discovered a way to lure the Malliac through the rift to their doom.

He stopped in his tracks and smacked himself on the forehead.

It was so obvious to him now what the cynosure was.

It didn't lead to a weapon. It was a trap, and he had the beginnings of an idea of how to use it as such again.

"OKAY, KAINE," SAID Pavlovich, "I hate surprises, and I've had a bellyful of them for one lifetime. Before the others arrive, I want to learn what this little impromptu meeting is about."

Hayden couldn't shake his sense of dread as he worked up the courage to begin a conversation he didn't want to have.

"Captain, I know what the cynosure device is. It's flypaper."

Pavlovich eyed him with concern. "Do I need to relieve you on medical grounds, Commander?"

Hayden forced a reassuring smile. "I'm fine. Let me explain. I believe the Glenatat records have been mistranslated. I had Cora—"

"Is she back online?"

"Uh, yes, sir; about twenty minutes ago."

"And you didn't think it important to tell me?"

"There's not a lot of time, Captain. I needed her to retranslate the records to confirm my theory, and I didn't want her distracted."

Pavlovich glared at him. "Lucky for you the world is coming to an end. I'll grant you some latitude, but this better be good."

Hayden smiled. "Cora, are you ready?"

"I am, Commander."

Pavlovich's face softened at the sound of her voice. "Welcome back, love. You had me worried."

"That makes two of us, Cap'n. The XO is correct that the Glenatat records were mistranslated. I reexamined them in the light of what we've discovered, and they all agree with his theory."

"The flypaper one?"

"The cynosure portal was designed to be activated within an enemy's star system. The power source they used would have been a planetary core, or the system's sun itself. It allowed an opening to be generated that was several AUs across; large enough to capture entire planets, or even suns."

"So, they just plopped this thing along the orbit of a planet they didn't like and let it ride inside?"

"It was diabolically effective, eliminating the home world of any enemy," said Hayden.

"Do we know how often they deployed it?"

"Not from the records," she said, "but we can infer from what we saw here that it was used at least three times: once to swallow a star—that was probably their first successful test. After that, up to twice more to capture the planets we found."

"There is also a theory we have that they captured the star to allow the inhabitants of those worlds to survive," said Hayden.

"An ingenious weapon," said Pavlovich. "Any ideas why they abandoned it?"

"It is possible they discovered the weak point we triggered and deemed further use of it too dangerous," said Cora.

"It sounds more like a tiger pit to me than your flypaper analogy."

"With enough power, it could be," said Hayden. "Presently, however, the device is being powered from Thomas's asteroid by a nuclear reactor. That gives it limited size potential."

"Okay, while I appreciate the background information, I think I know what your idea is. If we can relocate the portal in front of the Malliac fleet, we can trap them inside."

"No, Cap'n, that isn't possible," said Cora.

"Why the hell not?"

"Because once we close it, the next time it opens, we will face the same fate that threatens us now. Right now, I've gathered enough data to predict the current rate of collapse. We have time to get out of here, with some to spare. If we close and reopen the portal, however, everything changes. The inner protective bubble will expire immediately, and there will be nothing to prevent our universe from falling through the rift."

"Then how do you propose to use it as a solution?"

Cora hesitated, and Hayden looked at the captain.

The door opened, and Stella entered, accompanied by Katie.

Hayden's heart dropped into his stomach. Stella doubled over from the intensity of the emotional wave he sent out. He rushed to her aid and led her to a chair.

She looked up at him, pain etched on her face. "You hurt so much. What has happened?"

He could barely see her through his tears. "I'm so sorry, but there is no other way. I tried to find one, but..."

"What the hell is going on, Kaine?"

"Cap'n," interrupted Cora. "The Commander had me run through several thousand alternative plans. This is the only one that has a chance of success."

"I haven't heard a plan yet."

Comprehension came to Stella's eyes as she stared into Hayden's. "You need me for something you don't want to ask of me."

He nodded as tears flowed down his cheeks.

She reached for his hand and squeezed it. "Tell me what it is."

His voice cracked as he spoke. "We need to keep the portal open long enough to lure the Malliac fleet into it."

Pavlovich's eyes grew wide as he looked from Hayden to Stella. "My god, man! You intend to use her as bait."

Katie broke her silence. "What do you mean by that?"

"When I was a child, hiding from them at Mu Arae, I learned that my empathic ability gives me a strong connection to the Malliac. They seem to be instinctively drawn to me."

Katie appeared skeptical. "Do you know why?"

"They are attracted to emotion, especially fear. They feed on it, and for them, it is like a drug. My ability amplifies it, making me a potent source."

"How do they make use of it?"

"We don't really care to find that out." Hayden was annoyed that Katie's professional curiosity made her come across as insensitive.

"What is the plan?" Pavlovich didn't sound enthusiastic.

"Stella would be stationed in my shuttle just inside the entrance to the portal. *Scimitar* will FTL jump into the heart of the battle and assist the Earth defenders to redirect the Malliac fleet toward her. Hopefully they will sense her and be motivated to cooperate."

"Don't worry," she said, "they will be."

"How do you propose we rescue her?" asked Pavlovich.

"This is the dicey part. When the Malliac are redirected, we will hop ahead of them to retrieve the shuttle. When most of them pass through the portal, we will jump out, and Thomas will cut the power to the cynosure device, trapping them."

"Holy shit, Kaine. This plan can go sideways in so many ways. For starters, you will never get the entire Malliac horde inside before they realize it is a trap."

"I've run the simulations, Cap'n," said Cora. "Only seventy percent of their fleet needs to be trapped. Earth has the resources to repel the remainder."

"Still, that entails a huge risk," said Hayden. "We'll have to remain inside the bubble until the last possible moment."

"*Scimitar* will take a pounding like never before," said Pavlovich. "We may be destroyed or disabled long before the requisite number of enemy ships enter."

"Sir," said Cora soberly, "there is almost no chance that we will survive this."

Silence hung over the room.

Pavlovich spoke. "I'd like to give my crew an opportunity to volunteer for a risky mission like this."

"That's not possible this time," said Hayden. "Cora has been weakened."

The captain frowned. "Is this true?"

"Yes, Cap'n. Since my experience on Titan, my ability to monitor operations has been compromised. Most systems have gone unattended while I've been engaged in these simulations. I can run ship functions under routine conditions, but in a battle, I won't be effective."

"We will need every crewman at their station during this operation," said Hayden, "and every Ranger needs to be prepared to defend *Scimitar* when we are boarded. We can't afford to be shorthanded on this one, sir."

Pavlovich turned to Stella. "You're not military. I can't order you to do this."

Her face was wan. "You don't have to. There is no other choice."

"You're sure about this?" He looked from face to face.

"Yes, Cap'n," said Cora. The rest of them nodded in agreement.

The captain straightened his back as if summoning up the required strength. "Very well, make preparations. I shall inform the crew. Doctor, someone will have to coordinate with your grandfather. I'd like you to attend to that."

"Our tight beam comm link is still not working, Captain."

Pavlovich nodded. "It will when we exit the portal. After our jump, you will launch in our remaining drop ship to return to base and oversee the shutdown of the cynosure device. You know first-hand what is at stake here. I don't want somebody to let doubt prevent them from acting when the time comes."

She glanced between him and Hayden. "You can rely on me."

Hayden lingered until the rest of them had departed.

"Cora, I owe you my gratitude for not telling anyone about my rash act. I intend to face up to it if we survive, but the others don't need to have doubt or resentment going into this."

"You have nothing to apologize for. I was wrong. If you had not sent that message and triggered the collapse, we would've returned and faced a hopeless situation. The Malliac would have prevailed. With your act, you have initiated events so that humanity now has a chance for survival. If I can give my life for this to succeed, I will count it as well spent. I know the others would feel the same way."

"Thank you for saying so, Cora. I really should tell Stella, though."

"I know her well enough to tell you that it won't make a difference to how she feels about you. But it might distract her from what she must do. I counsel you to wait until this is finished."

"Thanks. I hope we have an opportunity to have that conversation."

But he knew in his heart that was not the case.

They would likely all be dead in a few hours.

Sacrifice

HAYDEN ENTERED THE hangar to the sight of Stella and Cora's engineering avatar engaged in a deep conversation. His heart in his throat, he approached, and they ended their discussion as he drew near.

"I tweaked the engines and installed some field enhancers to support the ship's armour," Cora said to him. "I wish there was time to install a dark energy weapon."

"I'll be fine," said Stella. "I have a few tricks up my sleeve."

"Just make sure you keep some distance from them as they enter," said Hayden. "We'll be right on their tails and will reach you first."

She smiled. "I know the plan, Hayden."

"I wish I could go with you."

"You can't, and besides, you'd just be a distraction I don't need."

"Umm, I also installed the other thing you requested, Stella."

He raised an eyebrow. "What other thing?"

"I asked Cora to install a self-destruct device. The last thing I want is to be taken by those monsters."

Hayden nodded; the nightmares she experienced when they first met were still fresh in his memory. "We'll be back before you have to activate the countdown."

"You're sweet, but we both know everything is out of our hands at this point."

"We're approaching the portal," said Cora.

She moved in and embraced Stella in a tight hug. When they disengaged, Cora turned to Hayden. "Her launch is in three minutes. I'll talk to you on the bridge."

Cora's android exited the hangar, leaving him and Stella alone.

"I wish we had more time," he said.

"Me too."

They stared at each other, at a loss for words.

A kiss and a final lingering embrace later, she boarded the ship and Hayden left to watch her departure from the observation platform.

As the shuttle lifted from the deck, all the things he wanted to tell her flooded his brain. He wondered if they would ever meet again and caught himself wishing he'd been raised in a religious faith that held the promise of an afterlife.

Wiping tears away, he left to join the captain on the bridge.

"WE ARE CROSSING THE portal barrier, Captain," announced the helmsman.

"Give me a tactical summary, Kaine. Where is the Malliac fleet?"

Eyes glued to his readout, he said, "The central concentration of their ships is nearing Neptune's orbital defensive perimeter; approach vector of forty-one degrees above the ecliptic."

"Have our forces engaged them?"

"No indication of battle taking place."

"Then we haven't missed the party."

Pavlovich turned to Katie. "Get to your shuttle. We'll be making our first jump to drop you off in ten minutes."

"Uh, fifteen, sir," said Chin from his engineering station.

"What's the delay?"

"The chief engineer is inspecting the FTL engine."

Scowling, Pavlovich hit the comm switch. "Cora, we don't have time for fiddling."

"The distortion front created some instabilities in the core, Cap'n. Unless you want to arrive with your leg sticking out of someone's head, I need to balance this drive."

"Why am I hearing about this now?"

"I told you, sir. I can only be in one place at a time. I'll call you when everything checks. I gotta go."

The comm channel closed on the heels of her comment.

"Son of a bitch!" A vein bulged along the captain's temple. "We'll stick to the rest of the plan. Kaine, is the tight beam link active?"

"Yes, Captain."

"Please call ahead and give the admiral a brief summary of our intentions, as we discussed."

"Captain, I'm detecting signs of weapons fire at the engagement front."

Growling, Pavlovich hit the comm switch again. "Cora, how much recharge time will we require after our first transit to drop off the doctor?"

"If we baby it, five minutes."

"And if we dump and jump?"

"The new balancing field won't have any time to regenerate. Everyone will need a barf bag, just like before."

"It can't be helped. We have to get into that battle. Finish fiddling, Cora. We're leaving."

He cut her off in mid-objection and turned to Hayden. "Damn it. This place was just starting to smell good. Sound general quarters. Make ready for FTL jump in two minutes."

He turned to Katie. "Good luck to you, Doctor."

"To you as well, Captain."

After a glance at Hayden, she left the bridge.

Two minutes later, *Scimitar* vanished and instantly reappeared a few thousand kilometres from Thomas's base. When Katie's drop ship cleared the hangar, Pavlovich paused only long enough to let her put some distance between them before he ordered *Scimitar* to jump again.

"Captain wait!" shouted Hayden. "Two Malliac scouts just showed up on our sensors. They are converging on Katie's shuttle at high acceleration."

"Are any of our ships in range?"

"No, sir, and the base's weapons don't appear to be online. They caught us off guard."

"Bring our cannon online. Plot and execute an FTL jump to put us between the shuttle and those marauders."

Seconds later the air crackled around Hayden, and the fabric of space distended as the drive activated.

Everything sprang back to normal in an instant, and he fought to keep his stomach contents down.

Without warning, the deck lurched beneath his feet and the entire ship shook. Hayden's weight shifted until he was pulled across the bridge to slam into a bulkhead.

He watched as the helmsman, who had the foresight to strap himself in, fought with the controls to bring their spin under control.

"What the hell was that?" yelled Pavlovich.

Rubbing the growing bump on his head, Hayden returned to his console and reviewed the sensor logs.

"We materialized in the path of one of the Malliac ships. It hit us with a glancing blow, and the impact appears to have destroyed it."

"Where is the other one?"

Hayden desperately widened the scan range until he picked up the second vessel. "It looks like it has broken off pursuit of Katie's ship and is making a long turn back toward us."

"He's no dummy," said Pavlovich. "He thinks we are disabled and intends to take us off the board. Ready the dark energy weapon."

"Captain," called Hayden. "The crash discharged the capacitors. We need to recharge."

"How long?"

"Another thirty seconds."

"Shit! He'll be on us before that."

"I have an idea," said Hayden. "Cora, cut power to everything except the weapon. Helm, stop compensation for spin."

"Let him think we're hurt and draw him in," said Pavlovich. "I like it. Do as Kaine told you."

Hayden's eyes were glued to his readout. "It's working; he's slowed his approach."

"He's taking a good close look at us. Gunnery officer, stand ready to fire on Kaine's command."

Hayden watched as the alien reduced his speed further. "Come on, come on," he muttered under his breath as the Malliac vessel crept closer.

"He's in range. Fire!"

The lights dimmed as the weapon activated. The dark energy beam tore through the front of the Malliac ship, sending a distortion wave down the length of its hull before the vessel exploded.

"Direct hit. Enemy destroyed."

"We've drawn our first blood," said Pavlovich. "Secure for jump. Get us into that fight."

Into the Breach

HAYDEN WIPED THE VOMIT from his chin and turned his attention to his instruments. He was glad he had the presence of mind to puke on the floor instead of his console.

"Everybody look alive," yelled the captain, his face pale and a sheen of perspiration on his forehead. "Where are we?"

"The battle is one hundred thousand kilometres off of our port bow," said Hayden.

"What the hell? Helm, I thought you were going to drop us into the thick of things."

"We couldn't risk materializing inside one of the other ships, sir. Given the activity in the area, this was the safest location."

Pavlovich ordered the ship to accelerate to the battle.

Scimitar streaked toward the conflict. Hayden monitored the situation as they approached, and what he saw made his courage flag.

The entire enhanced Earth fleet was deployed across the path of the approaching Malliac horde. A little over eight thousand UEF transponder signals registered on his instruments; virtually every ship available to humanity was involved in this last hopeless act of resistance. Sensors could not give him an accurate count of the enemy vessels, their dark matter hulls unresolvable as individual ships from this distance. There were well over a hundred thousand of them, spread out like an unimaginable swarm of bees. The writhing core of the mass was at least fifty thousand kilometres long and two thousand thick at its centre. Travelling at one quarter the speed of light, they had decelerated considerably from their near luminal interstellar transit velocity.

Hayden transferred a computer-enhanced hologram to the main viewer.

"The fleet has engaged the vanguard of the horde with long-distance, dark energy weapons."

225

Everyone's eyes were riveted to the unfolding scene. Still six hundred thousand kilometres away, the Glenatat-designed armaments were devastatingly effective, destroying thousands of alien vessels in a withering barrage.

Still, it seemed as though they swung a fly swatter at a cloud of mosquitos. While many of the leading Malliac ships were eliminated, a significant percentage evaded the human weapons and descended on the fleet.

To Hayden's great relief, the UEF forces presented a formidable resistance. Their attackers inflicted less damage than they were dealt.

"So far, the fleet is holding its own," he said. "Their weapons and armour are superior to what most of the Malliac ships appear to have."

"They're outnumbered by twelve to one," said Pavlovich. "They'll burn their weapon emitters out before the central wave of the enemy overwhelms them."

"What difference can we possibly make?" said someone.

Murder in his eyes, Pavlovich swung around in his chair, searching for the individual. Unable to locate the offender, he hit the comm button and addressed the entire crew.

"We will soon join our sisters and brothers who valiantly offer their lives for our species' right to survive. *Scimitar* will enter this fight and play our part, giving our lives if necessary. None of you were offered a choice. Nobody on Earth, or any of her colonies, was given one either. The Malliac do not care if we die willingly or cowering in fear. They only demand our deaths. We will not comply. They will pay a heavy price for this invasion. If you are religious, pray for our victory, then put all of yourself into your duty. Let them pry our cold, dead hands from our instruments and know that we did not give up. Godspeed to us all, and we'll share a drink together on this side of the veil or the other. Now, let's go get those bastards."

He pounded the switch to terminate the connection.

"I think that is your best speech to date, Captain," said Hayden.

Pavlovich turned toward the main viewer. "I hope I can remember it for my memoirs."

"The enemy will be in range in one minute," said the gunnery officer.

"Target the ones slipping through the kill zone."

Hayden's eyes were trained on the readouts, and as the mass of Malliac vessels began to resolve into individual ships on the sensors, it took him a moment to comprehend what he saw.

"Captain, the Malliac are holding heavy cruiser class ships in reserve. They're sacrificing thousands of smaller ones to drain the fleet's weapons."

"And Thomas fell for it like a rank amateur. Alter our course. We will take the fight through the centre of them. Signal the fleet of our intentions."

Hayden advanced to Pavlovich's side and handed a data pad to him.

"What's this?" He returned it, unread. "Just summarize it for me."

"The damage report is in. The collision created stress fractures in our starboard dorsal section." He pointed out the area on the pad.

Pavlovich grabbed back the device and studied it. "How badly compromised are we?"

"Cora is shoring up the damaged section with a gravity field but said we should try to protect that spot from any direct hits."

The captain's eyebrows shot upward, and he pointed at the hologram. "How does she recommend we do that while passing through that mess?"

"I think the rest of our hull will be in comparable shape or worse after we finish our first pass."

A grin spread across Pavlovich's face. "First pass, eh? I like your optimism."

He hit the comm button to again address the crew. "Look alive, people. We are going right up the horde's sphincter. The ride only gets rougher from here."

Moments later, *Scimitar*'s hull rattled as she encountered weapons fire on her approach.

"Cora has programmed an attack sequence based on sensor analysis," said Hayden. The deck shook beneath his feet. He gave the order for all hands to secure for potential loss of gravity, then strapped himself into his own chair.

Small escort ships protecting the central swarm exploded in brilliant flares as *Scimitar*'s dark energy cannon made short work of them.

"Save our powder for the big ones, gunner," ordered the captain.

Hayden called out, "Dedicate all firepower on the large vessels. The small ships can't penetrate our armour, but those big ones can do damage."

The ship lurched from bolts of enemy fire. The lights flickered but remained on. Hayden was pleased that he didn't detect any wavering of the gravity field.

They closed in on the first of fifty ships *Scimitar* was programmed to pass by. The bridge lights dimmed as the dark energy cannon siphoned power from the engines.

A destructive wave front engulfed the Malliac vessel, ripping it to shreds.

A cheer rang up from the crew. Hayden and Pavlovich exchanged looks of relief before they returned their attention to the next target.

Buffeted by increasing fire as they dove deeper into the heart of the swarm, *Scimitar* took everything sent at them. Ship after ship they encountered fell to their weapon, and Hayden began to wonder what had made the Malliac seem so formidable a foe.

A proximity alert came up on his panel, calling his attention from the attack run. He checked the reading then rechecked it to make sure he wasn't mistaken.

Touching his earpiece, he said, "Cora, I need you to look at these readings."

"Give me a moment, Commander. Chin needs some help with an energy surge in engine two."

Seconds ticked by as he waited for her. He only caught a glimpse of the thing before it became masked by the bulk of the horde, but it was unlike anything he'd ever seen before.

"Okay, Hayden," she said, "I don't have much time. What do you need?"

He informed her of his concern, and after a few seconds, an enhanced image came up on his screen. It showed a sphere, about a hundred kilometres across, almost completely black except for electric-blue plasma arcs surging along its surface like solar prominences. Thousands of Malliac ships were packed densely around it, as if protecting it.

"What the hell is it?" he asked.

"I don't know, but the radiation it is putting out is equivalent of a small sun, except it is dark energy."

"Is it a weapon?"

"If these readings are accurate—oh my!"

"What is it, Cora?"

"I have to check something. Stand by."

The comm link went dead, leaving Hayden with no answers and frustration building.

The ship lurched, pushing his shoulders against his seat restraints so hard, he was sure they would leave a bruise. Through it all, *Scimitar* continued to fire at every significant vessel they passed on their journey through the mass of Malliac ships.

"Hayden, I found something," said Cora in his ear, "and it's not good news."

"I didn't expect it to be. What is it?"

"Until I saw that thing, the Glenatat records didn't make any sense. That thing is a dark energy device designed to crack open a planetary crust like an egg. The Malliac feed on the geothermal energy of a planet's mantle."

Hayden could hardly believe what he heard.

The Malliac possessed a world-killer.

SCIMITAR passed out of the cloud of Malliac vessels, relatively unscathed, to the cheers of the crew.

"That's the first one, people." Pavlovich sounded relieved. "Make ready the FTL drive to put us in place for another run."

"Captain, wait!" Hayden unbuckled his restraint and hurried to Pavlovich's side.

"There is a bigger problem."

He explained about the sphere spotted in the middle of the alien cluster.

"It is putting out a massive amount of radiation. Cora thinks the energy signature looks remarkably like the quantum resonance spectrum of Stella's brain scan on file."

"You think it binds the Malliac together in this giant swarm?"

"It would explain a lot if it does. The ones we've encountered to date were separated from this thing and drawn to Stella in its absence."

"But with that thing in their midst, they won't notice the signal she's trying to put out to attract them now," said Pavlovich. "You said they were guarding it?"

"Their most powerful ships are protecting the device. They might even be drawing energy from it."

"We can't do this alone. Contact Admiral Thomas and inform him of the situation. He needs to deploy an attack force to break through the swarm and aid us in attacking the world-killer."

Kaine went to personally transmit the message. He returned a few minutes later, downcast.

"What did he say?" asked Pavlovich.

"He argued that he'll need to draw from the defensive perimeter to do that. More enemy ships will slip through."

"At best, he will delay the inevitable. When their weapons burn out, the Malliac will roll over them and carry that device to Earth."

"I told him that; I even brought Katie into the conversation to support my argument, but he won't change his mind. We are on our own."

"He's a desk jockey asshole. He just doomed the planet."

Pavlovich studied the progress of the battle on the bridge viewer. "How do things stand?"

"Fleet strength is down by fifteen percent. At the moment, our forces are holding the enemy to an advance of ten thousand klicks an hour, but the bulk of the swarm isn't yet engaged."

"How much time do you figure we've got before they ride over us?"

"Maybe forty minutes, assuming the Malliac don't bring some of their bigger ships into the fray sooner."

Pavlovich fixed his gaze on him. "What is your recommendation, XO?"

Hayden turned to the hologram to buy himself a few more precious seconds. His idea was reckless and the only thing he could think of.

"They will expect us to take another run at them. Sensors indicate the ships around the world-killer are repositioning to present a defence."

"So, running in like a berserker will not do much good, is that right?"

"Even with our armour, I doubt we can get close. Remember what happened at Mu Arae?"

"All too well," said Pavlovich. "But I see something going on behind your eyes. What is your idea, Kaine?"

"It's risky."

"We don't enjoy the luxury of being cautious. Spit it out."

He hesitated. "We use the FTL and materialize in the centre of the cluster, weapons at full capacity."

"We might make a lucky shot before they swarm us while our gun recharges," said Pavlovich.

"But that isn't the whole plan. We do several jumps in succession. Pop in, fire, jump out, and recharge. Then we repeat it at a different location."

Pavlovich stared at him, brow knitted together and jaw set. "Both require a lot of power."

"There are four engines, and for this, we won't need to generate much thrust. We dedicate the output to the light drive and the cannon."

"That sounds crazy, and I like it, which means Cora will hate it. Did you run it by her yet?"

"No, he hasn't, Cap'n, but the commander patched me into this conversation."

"That saved time. Will it work?"

"All engines are operational, but number three is showing some stress."

"Is it bad enough to negate the plan?" asked Hayden.

"No, but there is still the problem of the jump. The cluster of ships is so thick that it will be a gamble not to materialize inside one of them or collide immediately after we appear. Our hull is already showing stresses where we were hit by that other Malliac ship."

"We realize it is a risky plan, Cora. Can we make this happen?"

"I will program a series of jumps. I can compute our first arrival location based on our readings during the attack run. It will be the most dangerous hop because everything will have moved. Assuming we survive, subsequent runs should be easier because I can update the model from the sensor logs. Yes, Cap'n, we can make this work."

"Okay then, we've got a plan," said Hayden.

"There is one other concern, though," she said.

Pavlovich scowled. "Why is there always something? What is it?"

"The new dampening field on the FTL drive won't be able to keep up. Successive jumps will be hard on everyone."

"I'm not worried about a little puke."

"There is more to consider than the physical symptoms, Cap'n. Multiple transits without the compensation will affect the molecular integrity of both *Scimitar* and the crew, like it did before."

"How many can we make before we tear ourselves apart?"

"I really don't know. The process is nonlinear, and there are too many variables to predict. I can say for certain that the armour will be compromised, and there is a significant chance we will incur major damage. But even if *Scimitar* survives, we may not."

Hayden caught the fear on the face of the helmsman, who like most of the bridge crew had heard the conversation.

"If we don't do this, the Malliac will destroy the Earth, and humanity will be doomed. I don't think it will matter much if we live to see it."

"I don't believe there is another choice, Commander," said Cora.

Hayden lowered his voice so that only she and Pavlovich would hear. "There is also the degradation of Cora's system to consider. How long before the jumps become fatal to you?"

"I can't say. That is why I will program the jump sequence and make sure that all key systems are covered by my engineers. You should be able to complete the mission without me if necessary."

Hayden's heart was a lump of lead in his chest. The expression on Pavlovich's face told him he experienced the same. Given Cora's diminished condition since Titan, he was worried she might not survive too many FTL hops.

Grim-faced, Pavlovich gave the order to carry out the plan.

• • • •

Hayden thought his head would split open from the blaring klaxon, and the lights of the flashing alerts on almost every panel sent stabbing pain to the back of his eyeballs.

After six successive FTL jumps in less than ten minutes, no one any longer vomited, but like him, all showed signs of physical strain.

"Everyone take five." Pavlovich looked as bad as Hayden felt. "And somebody shut off that damned noise."

A perceptible wave of relief ran through the crew as the alert siren and accompanying flashing light stopped. The captain motioned him to approach so they could share a quiet conversation.

"We'll take a moment to pull our shit together before the next run. Give me a summary of our status."

Hayden swallowed down the last of his stomach's contents that rose up and tried to organize his thoughts. "With each jump, reaction times are slower. Everyone seems to be affected mentally as well as physically."

"Yeah, I'm feeling addle-brained too. How did we do on that last attack?"

"We caught them off guard on our first two jumps, but they were ready for us on this last one; we didn't manage a single hit on the world-killer."

"How much damage to it so far?"

"Cora is running a quick analysis on the sensor readings. We should receive an answer in a minute or so."

"Any idea how badly she is affected?"

"I don't believe she is any different, but you're familiar with how stubborn she can be. She may be concealing her symptoms better than us."

"I'm not hiding anything, Commander," said Cora. "I feel fine."

"Good to hear," said Pavlovich. "Tell me what you know."

"We hit them hard on our first attack, but since then, they drew their escort ships in tighter and made it harder for us to reach the sphere."

"Did our first two attacks do anything?" asked Hayden.

"I detected a power surge from it on our first strike, and its output reduced by twenty percent. But on the most recent runs the guardians took the brunt of our cannon fire."

"How is *Scimitar* holding up?"

"Hull held up well until this last jump. There are soft spots around our collision damage. I can reinforce it with a gravity field, but it won't survive a direct hit."

"We'll try to protect our wound. What else?"

She hesitated. "Cap'n, I don't think we can get at the machine. There are too many ships protecting it; our emitters will burn out first, or our hull could fail, or the crew could begin to suffer problems from the jumps."

For the first time, Hayden heard a strain in her voice. She was scared, just like the rest of them. The expression on Pavlovich's face told him he also noticed.

"Cora, take a moment." The captain's voice was surprisingly gentle, given the circumstances. "I know you; there is a solution you don't like, hidden in your back pocket. Tell us what it is and let me be the judge."

A pause followed. When she next spoke, she'd regained her familiar calm. "Yes, Cap'n. We will never penetrate the shield, but there is a consistent gap between the world-killer and the closest ship to it where the energy density is the highest."

"They probably can't approach without tearing their ships apart," said Hayden.

"That is my theory," said Cora.

"How big is this space?" asked Pavlovich. "Can we survive if we jump inside it?"

"It is only a kilometre and a half wide. We can take a lot more than they can, but I don't think we can last very long within the gap."

The captain stroked his beard in thought. "Can you compute how much it will take to finish that thing off?"

"We'll need to drain our engines in a sustained full-output burst."

"All of them?"

"Yes, and there is an impossibly small chance that we'll live through the subsequent blast if we manage to penetrate the object's exterior."

"So, it's a suicide mission with questionable odds of success?"

She hesitated. "Yes, sir. There is something else I should tell you."

"More bad news? Tell me."

"The prospect of us jumping successfully into that gap, with everything moving at one quarter light speed, is not good."

"I anticipated that. My question for you, Chief Engineer Symes, is can you pull it off?"

"You know the risks, Cap'n. All I can do is my best effort."

"Then that is good enough for me. Make your calculations and prep the weapon for maximum discharge. We are getting one kick at this."

Death and Mutiny

HAYDEN SLOWLY OPENED his eyes.

Scimitar was not buffeted by weapons fire and floated serenely in space. His headache and nausea were no worse than experienced in previous jumps.

What pleased him more was that he was still alive. The jump had proven successful. He thought he detected the collective relief of everyone and wondered if the sensation of connectivity was what Stella experienced.

He was pulled from his thoughts by Pavlovich calling for a report.

"We're inside, Cap'n." Cora sounded as relieved as any of them.

A hurried review of his panel confirmed her words. "The readings outside are like nothing in my experience."

"How is the ship holding up?"

There was a pause before she answered him. "Only minor FTL degradation of five percent, but the energy density surrounding the sphere is breaking down our armour. I estimate two minutes before the hull breaches, and everyone dies horribly."

"Can you reinforce it with another gravity field?"

"No, sir, we'll need every mega-watt to breach the sphere's surface."

Hayden brought up a hologram of the world-killer on the front viewer. A jet-black globe crackled with blue electric-like arcs running along it. The region around *Scimitar* was a milky mist, too thick to see the swarm of Malliac vessels surrounding them.

Pavlovich inhaled deeply. "All right, people. We'll only get one shot at this."

A high-pitched sound of rending metal ran over their heads from bow to stern.

"Cora?"

"Hull integrity is decaying rapidly, Cap'n."

"Then let's do this before we lose our chance. Gunnery Officer, target and fi—"

An explosion tore out a bulkhead.

Hayden watched in horror as half the bridge crew vanished, replaced by a gaping hole in the wall. The hurricane of escaping atmosphere seemed to want to suck the breath from his lungs as his seat restraint prevented him from following his comrades out into the void.

Remembering his decompression training, he exhaled. His desperate fingers clawed at his panel as he attempted to reroute the firing controls to it. He weakly croaked to Cora but couldn't tell if she answered due to the pressure building in his ears.

Almost as abruptly as it happened, the rush of air abated as the last of it was whisked into space.

He lost all sensation in his fingers as the plummeting temperature froze his flesh.

He only had seconds to live.

Through dimming vision, he reached for the controls and depressed the button to fire the weapon.

Then everything went dark.

• • • •

Every part of his body ached. The agonizing sting of blood flow returning to his extremities was the only thing that assured him he was not dead.

He felt pressure on his back and realized that he was lying down. His lungs burned with each breath, and he could see nothing but a white fog.

Voices found their way through to his still ringing ears as his clearing vision revealed shadows of people moving about and hovering over him. Finding strength, he tried to rise, but something pressed on his chest, keeping him down.

Slowly, his sight returned.

He was on the deck in the corridor outside of the bridge. Medical personnel attended him and others.

Trying to speak, his voice was muffled by the oxygen mask someone had placed on him.

"He's awake."

Hayden couldn't tell which of his rescuers still wearing emergency decompression gear spoke.

The familiar face of Cora's android appeared to hover over him, a look of concern on her synthetic face. "Thank God."

He struggled to sit up, recalling what had happened. "Pavlovich—"

Her hand firmly pressed him back down. "He's alive, though in worse shape than you."

Pulling off the mask, voice hoarse, he said, "How many?"

Her face grew sombre. "Three quarters of the bridge crew; sixteen others on two decks."

As more of his memory returned, he frowned. "Why are we still living? Did it work?"

"Yes, you activated the weapon. It took every bit of energy output from all the engines, but the beam breached the surface of the sphere. It's destroyed."

"Our damage?"

"Our armour mostly held up. We had three more breaches, but two were in the unoccupied crew quarter section. The explosion scattered or vaporized the escort ships. I consider our survival a miracle."

"The rest of the swarm?"

"They are still out there. They probably aren't attacking us because they think we're dead, which isn't far from the truth. And there is something else..."

"What? Did they roll through our defences?" He imagined the remnant of the Malliac fleet overrunning the inner solar system.

"No, but those that weren't near the blast changed course. They are heading for the portal. I think they sense Stella."

He sat up, brushing away the concerned efforts of Cora and the medic to keep him down. "What is our status? Are we capable of a jump?"

"Hayden, I know the plan called for us to return to retrieve her, but our engines are down. We can barely maintain life support."

"What about the FTL drive?"

"Operational, but there's no power, and the bridge is destroyed."

"Can't we run operations from another location? Engineering? How about from inside your VR?"

"Yes, I can construct a simulation and reroute the controls through it, but like I said, full power won't be available for another two hours."

"We don't need all the engines. We can operate everything from one. I'm familiar with the specs, so I know it can be done."

"Technically, yes, but that will only work under minimal requirements. The FTL will take everything an engine can output, and then there's manoeuvring, weapons, and environmental to consider. We can't operate with a single power plant."

"How long will it take the Malliac to reach the portal?"

"They were accelerating, so I'm guessing ninety minutes."

"Stella knows to retreat inside ahead of them." He looked up at Cora. "How much time to bring one engine back online?"

"I dunno; about an hour if I put everyone on it," she said, "but I told you we'll be useless in a battle with only one."

He slammed his fist into the deck. "Damn it! There must be a way."

Cora's voice softened, and she touched his shoulder. "Stella accepted the risks."

He glared at her. "*I* didn't. Think, Cora! Put that Glenatat technology keeping you alive to good use. Help me come up with a plan. Please?"

The expression on her android face hardened. "I *am* putting it to good use, running this ship and ensuring you and the others don't suffocate and freeze to death."

He couldn't look her in the eye. "I'm sorry. I didn't mean it like that."

"It breaks my heart too. I would do anything to save Stella. We are limited by physics and the technology—" Her mouth clamped shut and her eyes darted about, as if an idea had suddenly come to her. "Unless..."

Hayden rose to his knees, eyes locked on her. "What are you thinking?"

She hesitated. "If we think of this as a rescue operation instead of a combat one, there is a possibility we can make it work."

"Go on..."

She became excited. "I can run the engine directly. We can switch output as required: two FTL jumps, one to the gate and another to Stella's location inside the bubble once we locate her. We load her ship in the hangar then repeat the operation in reverse."

"Yes, yes. I like this."

Her expression hardened. "There will be no power for the weapon, and our armour is in bad shape. One well-placed shot, and we'll be toast."

"It is a risk I want to take."

She hesitated. "You can count on me, Hayden, but what about the rest of the crew?" She looked to the unconscious form of Yegor Pavlovich lying on the deck, covered with a thermal blanket and wearing an oxygen mask. "They paid a heavy price already. If we do nothing, the Malliac will enter the portal and the admiral will close it behind them. None of their lives will be risked."

Hayden looked around him at the injured and the rescuers. Cora was right. He had no right, or authority, to place them in further danger. "How many would be required to pull off a rescue op?"

"We need someone to run the operation and pilot the ship from the VR. I can keep the engine running; the two of us can do most of it."

"That doesn't give us much leeway. If anything goes wrong..."

"Then only some of us will die."

He stood and again surveyed the people in the corridor. "Will they be in danger if we order them to the life pods?"

A faraway look crossed Cora's face. "Most of the Malliac are now on their way to the portal. Only a few continue to engage our fleet. They should be safe—well, safer than what you and I plan to do."

"Pavlovich will be pissed."

She looked at him, tenderness in her expression. "*Scimitar* is his life. He would insist on coming if he knew what we have in mind."

"I'll order the medics to keep him under until he's safely off the ship."

"If we survive, Hayden, he'll want to kill you."

"He'll be welcome to try if I make it back."

"In all seriousness, you should think this through. Your military career will be over; you'll spend the rest of your days on a penal planet."

"Stella will be alive. I just wish I could do this without you. I'm sorry, Cora."

"Shut up, Commander. This is my idea, remember? Are we going to do this?"

He hesitated, running over all the considerations, worried he hadn't thought of something.

"Begin working on the engine. I'll give order to abandon ship once your team is finished."

· · · ·

"No, Commander, we're not leaving."

Hayden could tell that Chin's words didn't come from bravado. The determined expressions and nodding heads of the cadre of engineers standing behind him confirmed the truth of that.

"There is little chance of survival," he told them. "If you leave in the life pods, you'll be picked up by the fleet and make it home to your families."

Chin looked back at the group. More of the crew had entered engineering, and the growing crowd now spilled out into the corridor. He turned back to Hayden. "Commander, many of us are from the colony worlds. Our families are probably dead at the hands of the Malliac. If not, it would still be impossible for us to return to them without *Scimitar*'s jump drive. At the very least, we want to make sure she returns home from this mission."

Chin and the others knew that argument was weak. The FTL drive's plans were now in the possession of the UEF. Before long, improved versions of the technology would be available and the empire would be reconnected.

There was little doubt in Hayden's mind that, for the engineers, Cora was their reason for staying. As far as the others' motivation, he was not prepared to guess, but he suspected they all shared a fondness for Stella as much as a sense of loyalty to *Scimitar*.

A large Ranger, a head taller than the rest of the gathered crew, elbowed his way through the throng. He presented himself and offered up a crisp salute, which he held until Hayden remembered to return it.

"Commander, speaking for my squad, we don't want to leave our post. We all came aboard itching for a chance to kick some Malliac ass—begging the Commander's pardon—and the way we see it, you may need us before this is over. We request permission to continue our mission aboard *Scimitar*, sir."

Hayden surveyed the faces arrayed before him. Some were anxious, others determined. None appeared fearful.

"I take it you all agree?"

Heads nodded, and several shouted their approval.

He took a moment to consider it. "Very well, remove the wounded and attending medical personnel to the life pods. Anyone who wishes to join them is free to do so. Otherwise, return to your posts and make ready for FTL jump in twenty minutes."

A cheer rang up before the crowd dispersed as quickly as it formed, leaving a lone figure near the door. Pavlovich's eyes were bloodshot, and his pallid face seemed corpse-like in contrast to his bushy black beard.

"You look like hell."

He grunted and limped painfully forward. "You're one to talk, Kaine."

He towered intimidatingly over Hayden. "Well? Are you going to return my ship to me or what?"

"With all due respect, Captain, you're in no shape to command."

Pavlovich snorted. "Bullshit. Just because you recovered faster doesn't make you more fit to command than me." A wry smile grew behind his beard. "Besides, if you send me back to Thomas, he'll pin a stupid medal on me and declare you a mutineer."

Hayden smiled. "You'd let him, wouldn't you?"

"Damned straight."

He shook his head. "Very well, Captain. You look like shit, and I doubt you're recovered enough to run a book club, but I relinquish command to you." His grin grew and he added an exaggerated salute. "Sir."

"Don't be an asshole, Kaine. Let's get this show on the road."

A New Way of Doing Things

PAVLOVICH HELD THE VR helmet in his hands and looked around the conference table at his bridge crew. They were all reclined in their seats, helmets on and immersed in the simulation Cora had constructed.

He turned to Hayden. "You're sure this will work?"

He raised a questioning eyebrow. "Have you not done this before?"

Pavlovich turned the helmet and examined it. "I visited Cora's world a few times. It was weird."

"Stick with it. You'll become accustomed to the sensations after a minute or two, and then it will seem normal." He donned his own gear, and, after adjusting the fit, glanced up at the captain, who hadn't put his on yet. "Captain, do you wish to transfer command back to me?"

Scowling, he jammed the device onto his head, reclined, and closed the visor. Hayden chuckled to himself and followed him into VR.

After a moment of disorientation, a familiar scene materialized around him. The bridge crew were all at their stations, and the pings and beeps of the instruments filled the air. He flexed his knees, marvelling at how accurately Cora had replicated the sensation of the gravity plating. She even faithfully reproduced a weak area near one of the plate junctions. Amazingly, the smell of the place was the same.

"Wow," said Pavlovich from his command chair. "This is bloody amazing. I could swear I am on the real bridge. How did she do it?"

"I'm glad you like it." Hayden turned to see Cora, not having aged a day in a decade, sitting at the engineering station.

Pavlovich's expression quickly softened to a friendly smile. "I'm happy to see you again."

She grinned back. "Thanks, Cap'n, all systems are ready. Chin and his crew have engine two operating at ninety-eight percent efficiency. They've begun working to bring number four online."

"Uh, that's great." The captain was distracted and wiggling in his chair. He looked up, a critical expression on his face. "It doesn't squeak."

Hayden resisted the urge to laugh.

Cora smiled and replied, "I'll have to work on that, sir."

Pavlovich looked sheepish. "Well, I need to have confidence this simulation is accurate," he said, clumsily trying to recover his dignity.

Hayden forced a serious expression. "That is a very reasonable concern, Captain, but I am confident Chief Engineer Symes' attention to the operational detail is spot-on."

"Of course it is. Damned silly to be worried about a missing squeak. Especially considering how annoying it was."

"I couldn't agree more, sir. What are your orders?"

"Right, let's go through the checklist, shall we, Cora?"

"Engine number two is online, and the FTL is ready to spin up. Armour integrity is down to twenty-one percent, and the dark energy cannon is offline until we get the other engine running. All unoccupied sections of the ship have been isolated and vented."

"What will our manoeuvrability be like between the jumps?"

"We'll have access to attitude thrusters, and I'll be able to provide minimal power to the main drive to move us forward and for evasive manoeuvres."

"We can anticipate the Malliac will want to follow her after we recover Stella," said Hayden, "so the Rangers are suited up and prepared for any boarding action."

"Do we know anything about the advance of the collapse front inside the bubble?"

"No updated information beyond what Stella transmitted before she entered the portal." Hayden was concerned that she hadn't sent any updates but realized her attention was likely on other matters.

"Okay," said Pavlovich, settling into his seat. "Let's make this work. Activate the FTL drive and hang on to your virtual cookies, everyone."

• • • •

None of the usual sensations of spatial distortion or physical discomfort preceded the report from the helm that the jump was complete.
The only thing Hayden experienced was a faint, brief fluttering where
his stomach would be. Cora had obviously made provisions for the effects of the jump within the simulation, but he was worried that he
might yet emerge from the experience back in the conference room,
covered in his own puke.

"Where are we?" asked Pavlovich.

Instead of a holographic image appearing on the viewer, their surroundings vanished. Hayden panicked when he found himself floating
in space.

He heard the captain exclaim, "What the hell?" Concerned voices
of the rest of the bridge crew merged into anxious chatter.

"Sorry, everyone," announced Cora from somewhere. "We are all
still on the ship. I should have warned you about this."

"It's okay," said Pavlovich. "This is really cool."

Hayden looked about him at the immersive scene. Thousands of
Malliac vessels were distant specks, all vanishing into the maw of the
portal in the distance.

"How do I access the sensor data?" he asked.

A translucent screen appeared before him, showing all the familiar
outputs. "This could change the way we operate ships in the future," he
said.

"Agreed," said the unseen Pavlovich, "but let's not get ahead of ourselves. We still have to secure that future. Can we risk a jump into the
portal from here?"

"No," said Cora, "we have to pass through the opening in normal
space."

"Right alongside those bastards."

"Yes, Cap'n, but we have a plan for that."

An alert popped up before Hayden. "A Malliac vessel is approaching us at 0.84 light speed," he shouted.

"We're not here to play with him," said Pavlovich. "Helm, execute pattern sigma one."

The bridge and crew rematerialized around them as the klaxon sounded. He felt inertia tug him to one side as *Scimitar* rotated and the thruster fired.

"He's still gaining on us," said Hayden, eyes locked on the sensor readouts.

"Are any others joining him?" asked Pavlovich.

He checked, then rechecked the long-range sensors. "Negative, he's alone."

"Cora, can we outrun him?"

"No, Cap'n, we can't pull the acceleration needed."

Hayden's panel lit up with red. "They fired at us. Direct hit to the dorsal stern. Minimal damage." It felt odd not to experience the ship shaking under fire within the VR.

"Okay, make ready to execute the next jump."

Hayden's heart skipped a beat when the bridge simulation winked out for a fraction of a second.

"Cora, what the hell was that?" yelled Pavlovich.

"The power output surged. FTL drive is resetting."

"How long?"

"A couple of seconds."

Hayden's surroundings went dark, along with any sense of gravity or breathing. Just as suddenly, it reappeared.

"They hit us again."

"No shit," said Pavlovich.

"Cap'n, they're targeting a weak section of our armour. A few more like that and we'll be done."

"Punch the jump drive," he ordered.

"No can do, Cap'n. Every hit forces the FTL to reset."

"Shit! Can we redirect energy to the weapon?"

"Yes, but I'll have to transfer power to do that, leaving us at the mercy of momentum. They'll be on us before the capacitors charge."

"Damn it!"

Keeping his eye on the fast-approaching marauder on his screen, Hayden said, "Is the aft rail gun operational?"

"Yes, it is," she replied.

"Brilliant idea, Kaine," said Pavlovich. "Gunner, target that piece of shit and let relativity do the rest."

The Malliac ship blossomed into a blinding flare as the rail gun projectile's relativity enhanced mass drove through it at near light speed.

Hayden exhaled noisily and said, "Thank you, Doctor Einstein."

"If nobody else objects," said Pavlovich, "let's get ourselves to the mouth of that portal."

"Aye-aye, Cap'n," said Cora.

Pavlovich motioned for Hayden to approach. "That was the easy part. I hope you have some other tricks up your sleeve for what comes next, Commander."

"As do I, Captain."

Welcome Home

SCIMITAR's appearance among the mass of Malliac vessels streaming through the portal seemed to go unnoticed. Within the span of the few seconds when they might have been spotted, Stella's shuttle was located on the other side of the anomaly. The FTL drive was activated, and they vanished without incident.

"Holy crap, can I breathe now?" said Pavlovich before his demeanour returned to businesslike. "Report."

"We've jumped ahead of the Malliac swarm. They are twenty minutes out." Hayden scanned his instruments until he spotted what he was searching for. Not bothering to conceal his relief, he said, "I found her, two thousand klicks off the port side."

"Incoming transmission," said the communications officer. "Doctor Gabriel requests permission to come aboard."

"Granted," said the captain. "Open the hangar doors and orient us to receive her." He looked over at Hayden and smiled. "Tell her, 'Welcome home.'"

He turned to Cora. "How far away is the collapse front?"

She frowned as she spoke, her avatar not needing to access the virtual instruments on the bridge. "Readings are erratic, which we should expect when the laws of physics break down. My best guess puts it on top of us in fifty-seven minutes."

"Wow, that's cutting things close. Kaine, I think we can spare you for a few moments to say hello to Stella."

"Are you sure, sir?"

"Get the hell out of here. I want you back in five for the FTL jump."

Not daring to question Pavlovich's uncharacteristic generosity a second time, Hayden smiled broadly and terminated the simulation for himself.

• • • •

He pulled off the VR helmet, sat up, and took a moment to overcome the vertigo. Glancing down at his uniform, he was relieved he hadn't vomited during the FTL jumps, as he feared he might. From the smell in the room, however, it was clear that someone had not been so fortunate.

After dashing through the corridors, he arrived at the hangar just as Stella emerged. Seeing him, she ran to his arms.

"I was so worried for you," she said.

"I'm fine."

"The ship looks pretty badly beaten up. I wasn't sure what to expect. I didn't recognize the communication officer's voice. Whose was it?"

"A lot happened. I'll fill you in later, but I need to get back to the bridge."

"I'll join you."

"Um, that will be difficult."

"Why?"

Before he could answer, the deck shook, knocking them both from their feet. A second spasm moments later confirmed Hayden's worst fears.

He fumbled in his pocket until he located his earpiece. "Cora, what's happening?"

"We are too close to the collapsing front. Time and space are distorted. Some Malliac ships suddenly popped on top of us. The leading edge of it must extend to where they were."

Scimitar shook again under the barrage of enemy fire.

"Why didn't we jump?"

"For the same reason. The front is distorting everything. We have to put some distance between us and it."

The familiar vibrations and fluctuations of the gravity plates told him that *Scimitar* was under full thrust.

"I have to get back," he told Stella. "Medical is the safest place for you to be."

She nodded and started to go when the lights dimmed, and the tone of the klaxon changed. Seconds later, Pavlovich's voice filled the hallway. "Intruder alert! Rangers to sections D5, A3, and B1. All hands rig for multiple hull breaches. Commander Kaine, report to the bridge."

Stella's eyes were wide with terror. "It's me they want."

He grabbed her arm and pulled her along.

"Where are we going?"

"I'm getting a weapon."

When they reached the door, Stella doubled over and clutched her head. "They're close."

He input his access code, and they entered the armoury. Scanning the racks, he selected a firearm for each of them.

"Hayden, this won't do much good against the number that are coming."

"I consider it an insurance policy."

The high-pitched scraping of metal on metal ran along the outside of the ship over their heads.

Pavlovich's voice boomed over the speakers: "Pending breach at section C5. Rangers respond."

Hayden whirled around and grabbed two emergency decompression masks. Pushing one into Stella's hands, he shoved her toward the door. "Run!"

They were fifteen metres down the corridor when the deck shook, followed by an explosion behind them. He seized a handrail and wrapped his other arm about Stella's waist just before a hurricane of air rushed past them, threatening to pull them back through the hull breach.

Stella fumbled to put her breathing mask on as Hayden emptied his lungs so they would not explode.

An emergency bulkhead slammed into position, and the storm of escaping atmosphere stopped.

Gasping for air, Hayden rose and helped Stella to her feet. "That won't hold them for long."

As if to confirm his prediction, explosions thumped on the other side of the barrier.

Heavy, metal-shod footsteps approached from the opposite direction. Five heavily armed Rangers in full battle gear rounded the corner and came to a halt.

Without a word, Hayden pushed Stella toward them and followed as the sound of rending metal filled the air.

The soldiers activated mag-boots and fixed themselves to the deck in preparation for a pending decompression. Weapons raised, they trained them on the failing bulkhead in anticipation of what would come through.

Hayden pulled his mask on and shoved Stella back in the direction the squad had come from. As they turned the corner, an explosion was followed by another rush of air in their faces. Heavy weapons fire rose above the deafening din of the wind.

Another emergency bulkhead slammed into place behind them. Muffled gunfire and explosions could still be heard on the other side as he pulled Stella farther into the ship.

She reclaimed her arm. "Hayden, there are too many of them."

The fear he'd seen in her eyes since her first detection of the Malliac evaporated, replaced by a look of determination. She squeezed her eyelids shut, seeming to focus on a single thought. Her lips twitched in pain over her clenched teeth.

The sounds of battle ended.

Stella's eyes opened, and tears ran down her cheeks as she collapsed to her knees. "I'm sorry. I couldn't think of anything else to do."

Hayden rushed to scoop her into his arms. He kissed the top of her head and stroked her hair as he contemplated what he knew lay beyond the emergency barrier.

Stella had deployed the darker side of her gift she had used at Mu Arae ten years before. He had no doubt the alien intruders were dead, along with their compatriots still aboard the nearby ships. He was also sick with the knowledge that the soldiers who rescued them died, collateral damage of her devastating ability.

He made a quick tally from memory of how many on board still had their cortical LINKs. Most of *Scimitar*'s crew had them removed when they joined Pavlovich for this very reason, but the Rangers and anyone else not part of the ship's family had suffered the same fate as the Malliac.

He helped her to her feet. "You need to go to Medical."

"No, I can't remain on here."

"What are you talking about? We are one FTL jump out of this place. The portal will close, and the Malliac will be trapped here."

"No. *Scimitar* must still run the gauntlet through the swarm to reach the opening. They'll attack again and again to get to me, in numbers too overwhelming for me to stop. The ship is in no shape to take that kind of pounding. I have to leave."

He seized her shoulders. "No! I'll come with you."

Looking into his eyes, she shook her head. Gently, she grasped his hands. "Do you remember what I told you during the vote?"

It was like a lifetime ago. Tears filling his eyes, he nodded.

"This is my decision. It is my path; not yours. My sacrifice will have purpose, but if you come with me, your death will be meaningless."

"No, it won't. You shouldn't be alone. I can give you strength at the end; comfort you."

She squeezed his fingers. "No, Hayden; I've known for a long time that our destinies are separate. You are needed to rebuild. This is the purpose for which I was born. You must let me do this."

"But how can you know that? There may be some other way—"

She touched his lips with a finger and shook her head. "This is where our journey ends, my love." She pressed her palm to his chest. "I will be with you here."

Pavlovich's voice blared over the speaker, "Commander Kaine, report in if you are able."

Stella stood on her toes and kissed him on the lips.

Without another word, she moved away, slipping her hand out of his grasp.

Through tear-filled eyes, he watched her walk away.

After a minute of staring after her, he reached up and tapped the earpiece he still wore.

"Cora?"

"Yes, Hayden?" Her voice was gentle, as if she knew what had happened.

"Do whatever she asks of you, please?"

"Of course. Do you want me to tell the cap'n?"

"Wait until she's gone. Tell Pavlovich I'm on my way."

After a last lingering look down the corridor, he wiped his cheeks and straightened his back, steeling himself for what must happen.

He took a dozen steps before he stopped and sat on the floor. He needed to weep, and he didn't care if anyone saw him.

Stella

HAYDEN'S AVATAR REAPPEARED in the bridge simulation.

Conscious of everyone scrutinizing him, he went to his station.

"The ship is leaving the hangar, Cap'n." Cora's voice was quiet, her words hesitant.

When Pavlovich spoke, his tone was like someone forced to interrupt a funeral. "Comm, transmit the private message I gave you for her."

Even the communications officer, who barely knew Stella, choked up as he acknowledged the order.

"Mister Kaine?"

Pavlovich's voice tore Hayden from the thoughts that consumed him as he stared sightlessly at his console.

He straightened his back and replied, hoarsely, "Yes, Captain?"

"Are you able to monitor the sensors, or should I ask Cora to?"

"I'm fine, sir."

He needed to watch Stella's progress for as long as possible, intending to brand the images on his memory.

His eyes were locked on his instruments. "The shuttle's thruster is powering up, and the ship is accelerating. Heading..." He paused to keep his voice from breaking. "She's heading toward the advancing distortion front."

"What are the Malliac doing?"

"They are adjusting to intercept; they're following her."

"Good girl," said Pavlovich under his breath. "Helm, take us to the portal. If they decide to come our way, I want the engines to ramp up to maximum acceleration. We'll punch our way through. Comm, standby to send the coded signal to Admiral Thomas once we clear the gateway."

Hayden kept his eyes glued to the sensor readout, never allowing his attention to waver from Stella's progress. He was surprised that his avatar could shed tears as he wiped them away.

In the background, like an annoying buzz that could not be shut out, he vaguely paid attention to their own progress back to their own universe—one that would never again be the same for him.

An Offer Not to be Refused

HAYDEN SAT ON HIS BUNK and contemplated the bottle of rum. Sitting on the desk, it silently called to him to crack its seal and down its contents. It was the one Kyle had brought only a few days earlier.

With a heavy sigh, he pulled his gaze from the liquid temptation and perused the room he and Stella shared.

Her hairbrush was on the bureau where she'd left it. Her discarded clothing littered the floor as if nothing was different.

Tears threatened to fall, and he forced himself to laugh at her unkept promises to pick up after herself. Straightening up the room seemed like an act of desecration to him, so everything remained as he found it.

He hadn't even slept in the unmade bed. Instead, a pillow and blanket occupied a place on the deck next to it.

The door buzzer startled him, and for the briefest of instants, he wondered why Stella would have used it. As reality reasserted itself, his shoulders slumped and he called out, "Come in."

Kyle stood silent in the doorway for several heartbeats. His eyes drifted about the room before settling on Hayden.

"I thought I'd check in," he said. Hayden knew him well enough to realize the words were not as casual as he pretended.

"I'm fine."

Putting on an unconvincing smile, his friend entered and sat next to him on the bunk.

"Can I get you something?" he asked as his eyes settled on the bottle of rum.

Hayden grunted. "No, thanks. In fact, I was meaning to return that to you."

"Katie and I can't express how sorry we are—"

"Thank you, Kyle."

"We're all worried about you."

"All?"

"Me, Katie, Cora, Pavlovich, your uncle...even the admiral is asking about you."

"He just wants an answer from me."

"Have you decided what you'll tell him?"

"I really didn't give it much thought," he lied.

Kyle hesitated. "I realize it is a bit soon for you, but you need to begin thinking about your future. Stella wouldn't want you to—"

Anger flashed in Hayden's eyes. "How would you know what she would want?"

"Hayden, you've been holed up in this room for a week, have hardly spoken to a soul, and as far as anyone knows, had nothing to eat or drink. You have to take care of yourself. Stella didn't sacrifice her life so you could starve to death."

"I'm pretty sure she didn't die to ensure Thomas could assume control of the government again. Don't you think it was convenient how the existing regime just decided to step aside and let him come back as if nothing happened?"

Kyle frowned. "We both knew he had irons in the fire. The invasion was the pretext he needed to gather the necessary support."

"And now he is president again. Good for him; you too, I presume. As his prospective son-in-law, you will do well for yourself."

Kyle glared at him. "That wasn't fair."

"No, it wasn't, I'm sorry. I'm sure with Eli's mentorship you will make a fine attorney general. I mean that. You may be the most honest man in his cabinet, from what I saw."

"You have the ability to change that."

Hayden snorted. "Yeah, sure."

"I'm serious, Hayden. Most of Thomas's support is provisional. There remain a number of influential people still loyal to your father and willing to back you should you decide to oppose him."

"And risk ending up dead like Dad?"

"Don't be dramatic. Accept his offer and become the vice-president."

"Support the man who is supposed to have murdered my father? I'm positive Stella wouldn't like that."

"Then what are you going to do?"

"Who says I have to do anything? Maybe I just want to fade into the background, or..." He shrugged.

"You're not planning to do something stupid. Stella didn't give her life so you can kill yourself."

Hayden frowned. "Who said anything about suicide?"

"Then what?"

Hayden shrugged again. "I haven't worked that out."

"Right now, Thomas is giving you some private time to grieve, but he isn't patient. He'll want an answer from you soon. If you don't accept his offer, he won't be pleased."

"I told you, I'm in no space to make such a decision."

"Without support from you, he'll see you as a threat."

"You're trying to tell me that my life will be in danger. I know that."

"Please, don't do anything rash. With the Malliac gone and the Glenatat FTL technology in his hands, Thomas is ready to reconstruct the empire. He can make things very bad for you if you get on the wrong side of him."

"Like paint me as the villain who brought it all upon us. That thought hasn't escaped me either."

"Hayden, I'm worried for you."

He stood and placed a reassuring hand on Kyle's shoulder. Plucking the bottle from the desk, he handed it to his friend.

"Every regime needs its fall-guy, the person who can be blamed for all the bad from which the new government intends to rescue the public. I never put much stock in the idea of destiny, but Stella did. Perhaps this is my true purpose?"

"Hayden, don't..."

He laughed. "I'm just blabbering, Kyle. I don't know what to do. I still need some time."

"Give the offer some serious consideration." Kyle started for the door but turned around after a few steps. "You're wrong, you know. You still have an important role to play."

Hayden smiled. "You mean saving the universe isn't enough?"

Kyle raised an eyebrow. "The empire is being reconstructed. You can have a major influence on how things will change."

Hayden nodded. "I'll give it some thought, I promise."

After Kyle left, Hayden stared at the door.

"You're right, old friend. I do still have a purpose. It's just not the one you think."

Endings and Beginnings

"YOU'RE SURE ABOUT THIS?" said Pavlovich.

"I am if you are," said Hayden. "Or was it just the whiskey talking?"

The older man scowled. "You got me drunk on purpose. I meant every word I can remember."

Hayden smiled and turned to the android standing next to the captain's chair. "How about you, Cora?"

"You guys are my family. I've never been surer of anything."

Pavlovich surveyed the bridge, empty except for them and Chin, who occupied the engineering station.

"And how about you, Mister Chin? If you and your buddies come with us, you'll all be hunted."

"You forget that I was a raider long before you recruited me, Captain. If you all are intent on pursuing a criminal career, you're going to need some experienced cutthroats to show you how to do it."

"I'm glad you and the others decided to stay on—and that you can keep a secret," said Pavlovich with a grin.

"Do you think they'll come after us once they figure out what we've done?" said Cora.

Hayden said, "If I'm gone, I may not be a threat to Thomas, and he'll leave us alone. I doubt he wants to make a martyr of me."

"No," said Pavlovich, "he'll have to trash your reputation first. Then he'll put a price on your head—all our heads. I know the man well enough to know he won't rest until we're eliminated."

"Well, he'll have to find us first."

"With that said, have you selected a destination for us, Cora?"

"The modifications to the FTL drive give us a lot of leeway, Cap'n. I picked a nice little place for us to explore that is well beyond the edge of the empire."

"Does this place have a name?" asked Hayden.

"Nope, that will be up to the cap'n."

Hayden smiled. "Do you have any more books to inspire you?"

"I have an entire library in my quarters."

"Then what are we waiting for?" said Hayden.

Cora spun up the FTL drive, and *Scimitar* vanished.

Free book offer

Free eBook Offer!

As a way of saying thank you for purchasing this novel, I want to offer you a free ebook.

To claim your free story please join my reader list by going to

https://www.prudenauthor.com/Kaine1-free-offer

About the Author

D.M.(DOUG) PRUDEN WORKED for 35 years in the petroleum industry as a geophysicist. For most of his life he has been plagued with stories banging around inside his head that demanded to be let out into the world. He currently spends his time as an empty nester in Calgary, Alberta, Canada with his long-suffering wife of many years. When he isn't writing science fiction stories, he likes to spend his time playing with his grandchildren and working on improving his golf handicap.

Don't miss out!

Visit the website below and you can sign up to receive emails whenever D.M. Pruden publishes a new book. There's no charge and no obligation.

https://books2read.com/r/B-A-MNWD-IYQZ

Also by D.M. Pruden

Future Vistas
Future Vistas Vol 1

Mars Ascendant
The Ares Weapon
Mother of Mars
Child of Mars
Legacy of Mars
Mars Ascendant Box Set: Books 1-4

Requiem's Run
Armstrong Station
Phobos Station
Rhea's Vault
Ganymede Station
The Jovian Collective

Shattered Empire

Kaine's Sanction
Kaine's Retribution
Kaine's Reparation
Shattered Empire Omnibus: Books 1-3

Standalone
Throwing Stones

Watch for more at www.prudenauthor.com.